"Those two thieves back there in Kentucky, they meant to kill you didn't they, Shanks?"

"Sure did. Why else would they shoot me?"

"That's what I mean. If you had not put out their lamps, they sure would have blown out yours and given you a look at the pearly gates, that's for sure. I don't know about you, but for myself, I'd rather be sitting here telling the story than having them sitting in a nice dark bar bragging about blowing some dumb old nigger boy away to kingdom come."

Shanks took a bite off a chunk of dried sausage and offered it to Luke. "You know, I never thought about it like that," he said. "But you're right as spring rain."

Luke refused the sausage as he spoke. "Well, the same thing is true with the Indians. We are supposed to run them out. If it comes down to a choice between them and me, I can guarantee you I plan on being the one who tells the story."

Shanks laughed. "You're right, Luke. I never thought of it that way, but you sure are right. Me, too. I'm going to be the one who tells the next story, too."

THE BUFFALO SOLDIER

CHARLES R. GOODMAN

An Original Holloway House Edition
HOLLOWAY HOUSE PUBLISHING COMPANY
LOS ANGELES, CALIFORNIA

Published by
HOLLOWAY HOUSE PUBLISHING COMPANY
8060 Melrose Avenue, Los Angeles, CA 90046

This novel is a work of fiction. Names, characters, places and
incidents are either the product of the author's imagination or are
used fictitiously. Any resemblance to actual events or locales or
persons, living or dead, is entirely coincidental.

International Standard Book Number 0-87067-373-4
Printed in the United States of America
Cover art by Glen Tarnowski
Cover design by Bill Skurski

For Kendall and Jamie.
Two jewels that add sparkle
to Papa's life.

THE
BUFFALO
SOLDIER

Chapter 1

Luke took a small match safe from a shelf, then lit the first lamp inside the barn. Its yellow glow signaled a renewed vigil, a vigil that would go on for most of the night. There were three mares ready to drop their foals. Any one or all three could go into labor at any time. There was no doubt in his mind of the importance of each of these foals. Even though Luke was a slave, he knew the value of each newborn animal.

For the last several years, things had not been all that good at Red Oaks. Two years before, a fire had burned the cotton storage barn and Master Johnson had lost his entire crop. Since then, it had been one thing after another.

The rains came after planting this year and stayed. It had rained for almost the entire month. Luke knew most of the seeds in the ground would rot before they sprouted. If they could not bring in a crop this year, all the Master would have to sell would be some of his horses and these colts could mean the difference between "staying afloat or sinking" as Edward had told him.

All the lamps were now lit and the barn was cast in a yellow glow. Luke walked over to one of the stalls where a mare was watching him, her head sticking over the half door. He stroked her nose with his big, strong hand.

"You going to do it tonight, old gal? Give us a good stud colt?" He glanced over his shoulder to the door on the side of the barn as it opened.

Edward stepped through and closed the door. He pulled his hat off and slapped his leg with it to shake the water from the brim. "Doesn't look like it will ever quit raining."

"What you doing out here this time of night, Master Edward?"

Edward smiled, but did not answer. He walked to each stall and studied each of the three mares. Without turning, he asked, "Which one do you think will foal first?"

Luke looked at each mare, then went back to the first stall. He opened the lower door and stepped in. Slowly he ran his hand from just behind the front leg of the mare to about midway of her body. "Old Sugar here, Master Edward. She ought to have us a fine new stud horse before daylight."

"A stud horse?"

"Yes sir, I done asked her to give us a fine stud colt." He paused. "You done told me they bring more than a filly. Lord knows, ain't much of that cotton seed gonna pop up this year."

Edward walked to a table sitting next to the wall and pulled back a chair. He sat down and reached into his coat pocket. He brought out a pipe already filled with tobacco. He lit the pipe and exhaled a cloud of smoke.

"Ain't like you to come down here after supper, Master Edward. These here mares, they are gonna be all right. Me and old Ben, we ain't gonna let 'em out of our sight 'til we got three healthy foals up and runnin' around.''

Edward smiled. He knew Luke meant exactly what he had said. These mares were like his and old Ben's children.

"I know you and Ben will look after the stock and do everything that needs doing." He took another puff on his pipe. "That's not why I came down here tonight. I am going to be riding out early in the morning and I will need you to have my horse ready. I will need four or five days' worth of grain to take with me."

"Four or five days' worth?"

"That's right. I've got a long ride ahead of me."

Luke shook his head. He wanted to ask Edward where he was going, but he knew his place and would never pry or seem too inquisitive. It just was not accepted. Even though Edward had always treated Luke with a degree of respect, Luke knew the bounds and never crossed them.

Edward stood up. "Well," he said, "don't you want to know where I'm going that will take all that grain?"

"Only if you want to tell me."

"The Army. I have been granted a commission in the Army."

Luke looked up. "Army? You done gone and signed up in the Army? Man, your mama is gonna be fit to be tied. I heard her a while back yelling at you about the Army."

Edward laughed. "She was all worked up that day, I've got to admit." He turned to walk toward the door, then stopped and turned back toward Luke. "This is something I've got to do. She understands that now. I want you to look after her while I'm gone, you hear."

"Yes sir, Namdbi and me will look after her all right."

"That mammy of yours, you best keep an eye on her too. She hasn't looked too well lately."

"Namdbi, she's all right, Master Edward. I heard her say

11

to old Lois she just got the woman problem, that's all. She's gonna be all right."

One of the large front doors swung open. Standing in the middle of the doorway was a heavy-set, red-headed man. He was soaked to the skin. "Nigger, get your black ass over here!" he shouted.

Luke looked at Edward, then back at Overseer James. "Yes sir, Master James." Luke started to move.

"Stay where you are," Edward ordered. He stepped clear of the stall that had hidden him from view.

James was surprised to see Luke was not alone. "Mister Edward. I didn't know you were here." His voice had lost its arrogance.

Edward walked up and shoved James back outside. He reached out and closed the barn door and turned to face James. "You are drunk."

"No sir. I ain't drunk. Had a couple of drinks, but I ain't drunk."

"Now, you listen to me, James. That boy in there has got all he can handle with those mares. He doesn't need any of your crap. You hear me. You stay away from this barn and you stay away from him or I'll take that whip you keep to you. You understand that, mister?"

As Edward finished, he gave James a shove backwards. James lost his balance and fell. He started to get up, his fist clinched.

"Don't do it, James," Edward cautioned. "I've been looking for a reason for a couple of years to beat you to a pulp. You give me that option tonight and I'll pound you into that mud hole you are sitting in, then I'll fire you."

James pushed himself up. "You got no cause to treat me like I was one of them."

"Them," Edward's statement was firm, "is why people like you have a job. Them is why people like me make a

12

living. When are you going to get it through your thick skull that without them we couldn't run a place like Red Oaks. Now get yourself to your cabin and sober up. I am not going to tell my uncle about this, but you can bet your ass if I catch you drunk again, you are as good as gone."

James staggered off into the night headed toward his cabin.

"Almost wish I wasn't leaving in the morning," Edward said to himself. "That man has been a problem for as long as I can remember. Why Uncle Harry keeps him is beyond me." He reached the porch and turned back to look toward the barn. The yellow flickering of the lamps told him Luke was taking care of the only income Red Oaks would have this year.

Chapter 2

Edward had been gone for almost two years. From time to time, Luke's mother, Namdbi, would overhear some of a letter from Edward. She would tell Luke all she had heard, but he still knew little of the war or the fate of his young master.

"I wonder where Edward is now, ol' horse." His question was directed toward the mare he was feeding. "I suppose he's up north doin' his war with them yankees. Maybe he ain't comin' back. Maybe he done gone and got himself shot dead."

"What are you going on about, boy?" Overseer James said as he entered the barn. Luke turned to face James.

"Nothin', boss, just wonderin' about Master Edward to this here ol' mare. I talk to my horses all the time."

"Is that a fact now? Do they talk back to you, you dumb burr head? I been noticing you been doing a lot of wondering as of late. What did that horse say? That you're about the laziest thing it ever saw?"

James' voice had that sound Luke had heard before. The sound of bone-deep mean brought on by whiskey and just plain orneriness. James liked to hurt people. Pain inflicted on one of the slaves gave him great pleasure. Twice in the past month, Harry Johnson had dressed him down for a beating he had given to one of the field hands. Luke sensed that he was now at the wrong place, at the right time.

"I asked you a question, boy. That there horse — tell me, does she talk to you?"

Luke smiled and bowed his head as he shook it. "No sir, she don't talk, but she does listen good." He snickered as he finished. James staggered and bumped into a stall. Using the rails to steady himself, he glared at Luke. "You laughing at me, boy?" he demanded.

"No sir, I ain't laughing at you."

"Don't you lie to me, you ignorant black good-for-nothing."

James lunged at Luke. His big fist was aimed at Luke's face. Luke stepped aside and James almost fell to the ground before he regained his balance.

"What's the matter with you, Master James? I ain't done nothin' to rile you. I'm a good boy. I does my job. I never back talk to you. Why you want to put a hurt on me?"

James' shoulders slumped and, like a wild bull, he charged Luke growling like a dog as he lunged again, his hands outstretched as if to grasp Luke by the throat. Luke put up his own hands to ward off the attack. Luke twisted to one side and as he did, he gave James a shove. James fell into the nearby stall. He turned and Luke could see his eyes. They were the eyes of a mad man. His face had taken on the appearance of a wild animal.

James saw a hammer lying by the forge where Luke had

been working earlier. He picked up the small sledge and banged it on the anvil.

"I'll cave in your damned head, I will." As he shouted, he drew back to strike Luke. In his drunken stupor, he was no match for Luke. A bare foot caught the overseer in the groin and sent him crashing back, doubled up and moaning with pain.

The noise and shouts coming from the barn had attracted attention. Several slaves had run to see what was going on. Master Johnson had been on the porch and ran to see who was causing such a scene in his barn.

James had gotten back to his feet, hammer still held ready to strike. Luke grabbed the arm holding the hammer and with a turning motion, threw the drunken overseer half way across the barn. Johnson was now inside the barn. He screamed at Luke, "What's got into you! You crazy or something?" As he shouted, he drew the pistol he always carried and pointed it at Luke's head.

"Hold it right there. Don't you move a muscle or I'll blow your head plumb off your shoulders." In the excitement, the old man's voice cracked like that of a young boy.

James groaned and rolled over, holding his groin. "He attacked me for no reason. I just jumped him about being lazy."

"That ain't so, Master. He was gonna do me in with that hammer for no reason at all."

"Shut your mouth, boy. No matter what he was going to do, I can't have a slave of mine whipping up on my overseer. Jim, you and Clyde put Luke here in chains. I want him brought out to the post."

"Now wait, Master Johnson. I tell you Overseer James was gonna do me in, he was."

"You heard me." As Johnson spoke, he looked toward a short stocky slave.

"Yes sir, Master Johnson."

Luke put his hands up to ward off the two slaves approaching him. "I don't want no trouble." As he spoke he backed away. "I ain't never give you no cause to whip me."

"Best do what the master says, Luke. We don't want to hurt you," Jim advised.

A slave almost half again as big as Luke grabbed him from the rear. Luke submitted as his wrists were chained. He was then led outside to a post standing in the yard. There was a large ring near the top of the post. The chain was fastened to the ring. Johnson pulled off his coat and handed it to one of the slaves.

James came staggering out of the barn and approached Johnson. "Let me whip this one, boss. I owe him a good thrashing."

Johnson turned to James. "You're drunk."

"I may have had a couple, but I ain't drunk. Not so drunk, I can't skin this boy to the bone."

"I've told you before I would not tolerate drunkenness." Johnson's voice was firm. "Now get your things and remove yourself from Red Oaks. Because of you, I've got to whip one of my best hands. Now get out of my sight."

"You can't fire me, not like that."

Johnson turned to face James. His pistol butt was protruding from his waistband. James saw it as he spoke. "No sir, you can't just fire me. Not after all the years I've run this plantation. If it wasn't for me, you wouldn't have a plantation. Now, give me that whip."

He reached for the whip and Johnson reached for his pistol. Both men struggled. There was a muffled explosion. Johnson's head slowly raised skyward, his eyes rolled back and he slumped to the ground. James had the pistol in his right hand.

"Oh, my God! You've killed the master!" one of the women cried. One hand flew to her mouth, the other grasped her skirt as she ran toward the main house. James lifted the pistol and shot. The woman fell forward. Her momentum carried her face down in a cloud of dust.

A slave named Jim jumped from the crowd and grabbed James in a hammer lock. "You done killed Mayla! You done did her in!" he shouted as he twisted James' neck. The crack sounded like the report from Johnson's pistol. James' limp body fell to the ground next to Johnson's.

"What we gonna do now?" someone asked in a bewildered voice. "Get me down from this post," Luke demanded.

Three men released Luke. By now, Johnson's sister, Donna Ann, had come from the house to see what was happening. She was between the post and the porch when she saw the two white men lying dead. She stopped and screamed and turned to run back toward the main house.

"Catch her!" Luke shouted.

"Murder! Murder!" she screamed.

As she reached the steps, two men raced up to her and grabbed her by the arms. Swinging herself around, she pulled free and struck out with a clinched fist. The fist found its mark as her thumb gouged Black Henry in the eye. He released his grip and Donna Ann fell away. She staggered backwards and tripped on her long skirt. She fell and struck her head on the second step leading to the front porch. She lay motionless. A trickle of blood ran from under her head and down the step where a puddle began to form.

Namdbi raced to where Donna Ann lay and picked her head up with compassion. Her gentle fingers felt the limp neck for a pulse. She placed her ear on Donna Ann's chest, hoping to hear a heart beat. There was none. Namdbi looked up at Luke, who was now kneeling beside his mother. Tears were streaming down Namdbi's cheeks.

"She's dead, Luke. We've killed her. Oh, my God, what's gonna happen to us now? The master dead, his overseer dead, now Miss Donna Ann dead. Lord have mercy. They are gonna kill us all for this. I knew it was a bad day when that rooster sang his song last night. I knew it would be bad, but not this bad."

"Be still, woman. We have to think how we are going to get out of this mess. We didn't kill anybody. It just happened. That's all, it just happened. Now we have to save ourselves."

"She's right, Luke," Black Henry said. "They'll hang us all for this mess. Speaking for myself, I'm gonna run. If I get caught and hung, it ain't gonna be because I just stayed here waiting for 'em to come get me. Yes sir, I is gonna get away from this place."

"Where in the world you gonna run to?"

"I don't know, but I'm gonna get as far away from here as my feet will take me."

"Wait a minute. A plan is coming into my head." Luke stood up. His face had a blank look as if he was receiving a message from a long way off. "That's it! It'll work, too. I know it will work for sure."

"You got a plan, Luke?" Namdbi asked.

"I do. It will take all of us here to make it work. We have to stick together. Not a single one of us can go his own way. You hear me, Henry. No one can run on his own. We have to stick together if we are to get out of this mess alive."

"Tell us the plan, then I'll decide if I'm runnin' or not."

Luke looked around. All of the remaining slaves were present. Several had been sold in the past year. Red Oaks, like other plantations, was in financial trouble. Luck was with Luke since all of the slaves had been assembled for the whipping he was to receive. He could explain his plan one time and everyone would know his part.

"OK. We are all here. The master has a brother up north a ways. I was there a year or so ago to help him with his crop. Most all of us has been there some time or other, so you know where he is."

"We all know that. Some of us even worked his fields before, same as you. So what's that got to do with anything?" a tall, thin slave named Links asked.

"I'll tell you what. We are gonna load up three wagons with food and cottonfield things. We'll take us four riding mules. No horses, only mules. We strike a trail toward the master's brother and if we get stopped, we'll tell whoever stops us we are on our way to work the master's brother's fields, because his slaves ran off to yankee land. You have to let me do all the talkin'. Don't none of you open your mouth. I'll act like the overseer. I can scream at you same as he did."

Luke paused. "It's our only chance," he added.

"What we gonna do after we get to the master's brother's plantation?" Links asked.

"We ain't gonna go to his plantation. We're goin' to that yankee land ourselves. We are going to be free."

Luke stood up and his head sort of laid back, his eyes cast toward the heavens. "Yes, sir, we are going to be free, for sure. Now, you and you and you get the wagons hooked up. You women get some food out of the house. Get lots of dried sausage. There aren't going to be many fires. Now, get a move on. We don't have time to waste."

In less than an hour, they moved through the gate of Red Oaks. The three wagons came to a fork in the road several miles north of the plantation.

"Anyone know where that fork yonder goes?" Luke asked as he pointed to the right lane.

"That one goes to Jasper. I drove the master's wagon there once. It's a far piece, too. Maybe two, three days hard

21

driving," Henry said with authority.

"Two or three days, huh?"

"Yep, and I mean pushin' a team, too."

"Good. Henry, you take one of these wagons and you drive the fool out of it. You push this team all the rest of the day and all night if you have to, but you put some distance between you and this here fork. Take a ridin' mule with you. When you get a long way down that road, cut the team loose and cut across country and try to meet up with us. Hide your tracks when you leave the wagon. You hear?"

"Sure. But what about you all?"

"We'll tie brush behind the wagons and drag the road clean as we travel. After three or four hours, we'll cut the brush away. If we're lucky, we won't meet anybody. If we do," he paused, "well, we got us some guns under the sacks in yonder wagon. We'll fight our way to freedom if we have to. If we get killed, so what? We were good as dead back there anyway."

Henry nodded his approval.

"OK, you people in that last wagon, get yourselves up here in these two and make it snappy." He turned to Links, "I heard a fellow say that one time at the horse auction."

The road was seldom traveled and luck was with them as they drug the brush behind the wagons. Not a single traveler was seen. The three riding mules that were left rode point and their tracks were also wiped out by the brush. As dark approached, Luke spotted a dense growth of oak trees. The heavy underbrush would help to conceal them.

"We'll pull the wagons in there for tonight. Looks like it might come a storm in a while. We can get a little cover from those trees if it comes a hail."

"Lord, I hope Henry does what I told him to. If he don't, I swear I'll break his neck next time I see him," he thought to himself.

22

Chapter 3

Roger Boddy stepped out of his office door. He stood for a second and lit his cigar.

"Come on, Dave, let's go on out to Red Oaks and see if old man Johnson is ready to sell me that big bay stud horse he's so proud of. That old man is hard pressed for cash. The time may be just right to get him to agree on a price."

A tall, thin man rocked forward in the chair he had been sitting in propped against the wall.

"Mr. Boddy, that old man ain't going to sell that horse. He's sired too many good colts."

"He'll sell him. I just got word his nephew was killed some time last month. He'll be so upset I'm betting I can get him to make a deal."

"You saying he ain't got the word yet about that boy?"

"Nope. He ain't. Colonel Thomas just sent me a letter and asked if I would advise the family." He placed a foot in the stirrup and pulled himself up into the saddle. "Now, with Edward dead, that old man ain't got no heirs except for his sister. And Donna Ann ain't no spring chicken herself. Yeah, Dave, this time I'll get me that stud just as sure as night is dark. I'll have him in my barn come daylight tomorrow."

The two men rode in silence for almost an hour. The coming storm could be seen building in the southwest.

"If that storm hits, we might just have to spend the night at Red Oaks," Dave Roeman remarked.

"Well, I hope not. All I want to do is give that old man the message and get my stud, then get myself back to town."

Dave shook his head. He thought to himself, "I've known a lot of sorry people in my time, but this man takes the cake. Playing on that old man's grief to get a stud horse. That's pretty low even for Boddy."

The ride had now taken the better part of two hours, when Boddy remarked, "Wonder what ever possessed those Johnson's to put their place this far from town."

"They got good bottom land at Red Oaks. I suppose the nearest neighbor is at least four miles away and that's old man Turner. Might as well not have any neighbors the way he keeps to himself."

Again silence prevailed. Then Boddy shifted himself in the saddle. "Won't be long now. Just past that thicket and we'll see the house."

"Yep, and you got to tell Mr. Johnson and Miss Donna Ann about Edward."

"That won't be a problem. I never did like that boy anyway." As Boddy spoke, he lit another cigar.

The two men turned onto the lane leading toward the house when a bolt of lightening followed closely by an explosion of thunder caused both horses to jump and dance around.

"That was close," Boddy said. "Let's get up to the

house.''

As he spoke, he kicked his horse into a gallop. Dave followed close behind. Before they reached the main house, the rain started.

Their clothes soaked with rain, the men tied their horses to the rail. Once on the porch, Boddy turned and looked around.

"Funny. There aren't any slaves around. Should have been one to take our horses to the barn. Just like those lazy boneheads not to get out in the rain. If they were mine, I'd strap every one of them for not meeting a guest.''

Dave Roeman raised the large knocker and banged it on the door, then stepped back. No one came. He repeated his action.

"Good-for-nothing slaves,'' Boddy grumbled. "Go around back. They are probably all in the kitchen eating old Johnson out of house and home.''

Dave turned up his collar and walked to the edge of the porch then darted toward the back of the house. Boddy waited.

"What in the blue blazes is taking him so long,'' he remarked as he picked up the knocker and banged it hard against the door. He followed with a shout, "Hello in the house. Anybody home?''

The door opened. There stood Dave Roeman. He was as white as a sheet.

"What are you doing opening this door?'' Boddy asked as he stepped inside. Dave had a small derringer out and cocked. Boddy saw it and slid his hand to his waistband where he kept his handgun. "What's wrong with you? What's going on here anyway?'' he asked.

"I don't know, but there ain't nobody downstairs and there's blood here.'' He pointed at the floor just inside the door. "Look. There, it's leading to the stairway.''

Both men moved toward the stairs and started up when a clap of thunder shook the house.

"Good Lord!" Boddy shouted. "Did that hit the house?"

"I don't think so, but it was a mite close."

Using caution they reached the landing. The blood was now in a puddle that had dried, instead of the drops they had been following. Slowly Dave pushed a bedroom door open. He glanced around the opening. He stepped into the bedroom as his eyes searched every inch of the room. Nothing out of the ordinary. He backed out into the hallway. Boddy was now at the second bedroom. He turned the door knob and noticed there was blood on it. He shoved the door open and jumped into the room at the same time. He fell to the floor and rolled, coming up on one knee ready to shoot. He saw a body lying on the bed. He raised up and crossed the room. Dave now had entered the room.

"It's old man Johnson," Dave said.

"Shot right in the gut. Been dead some time, too. Maybe as long as yesterday."

"What about Miss Donna Ann?" Dave asked.

Boddy shook his head, then motioned with his pistol to check out the next room. The door swung open and there lay Donna Ann on her bed. Her hands were folded on her waist and placed in them was her bible.

"The slaves have killed everybody here. What is that crazy overseer's name?" Boddy asked.

"James something. James McGall, I think, or something like that. I'll bet you we find him dead, too. This place is just too quiet. I'll bet there ain't no one around. I'll bet those slaves killed everyone and took off."

"Maybe so. Let's check out the overseer's cabin."

"Wonder where he could be, if he's not dead?" Boddy questioned.

"Don't know, but I got to use that privy. I done gone and

26

got me a pain and I got to go bad.''

Dave opened the privy door, started in, and then backed out. Without turning, he shouted, ''I found him! I found the overseer!''

Boddy ran and looked in. ''Well, I'll be. They shoved him through the seat.''

''We got to get to the sheriff and get a posse after them murderers.''

''Yeah, we do, but we aren't going anywhere as long as this storm is going on. We won't be able to get back across Button Creek the way this rain's coming down. We'll spend the night in the barn. Come morning, we'll take my stud back in and report this killing then. Now, get some food out of the kitchen and meet me at the barn. They better not have hurt that stud horse or I'll hang every one of 'em myself.''

Boddy pulled his hat down over his eyes and ran toward the barn.

Dave tried to sleep, but found it eluded him. Each time he would doze off, he would see the two pale bodies lying upstairs in the main house. He couldn't help but wonder what had taken place that would cause such a thing to happen.

When morning came, the storm was over and sunlight streaked the eastern sky. Boddy had curled up in a corner and slept most of the night. Once he was sure none of the slaves were on the plantation, his fear was gone. The stallion he so badly wanted was safe in his stall. He knew the three dead people could cause him no harm and in a couple of days the slaves would be caught and hung. Before he fell off to sleep, he had devised a plan that would permit him to wind up with his sought-after prize.

''Well,'' Boddy said as he stood up and stretched. ''Put a couple of sticks on that fire and get me some coffee boiling. We need to get into town and report this killing.''

Dave stoked the fire and set a pot of water over the coals.

27

Sitting on his heels, he looked up at Boddy. "Don't it bother you none that three people are dead here? Their bodies are still lying out there. I mean old James even got shoved down in that pit." Dave stood up. "Don't it bother you, Boddy?"

"Watch your mouth, boy. You still work for me and if you know what's good for you, you'll do just what I say you do. Don't get me worked up or I'll run you plumb out of this state. May even tell the sheriff it was you that did those killings."

Dave quickly realized his position. Jobs were few and far between and he knew it was not beyond Boddy to lie to the sheriff if it suited his needs. He smiled as he slowly squatted down and added coffee grounds to the now boiling water. "Hell, boss, I suppose those dead people got me all worked up. Must have lost my head there for a second."

"Yeah," Boddy said as he reached for an empty cup sitting on a stool. "I suppose they would, if you let 'em. I didn't kill them, had nothing to do with it, so I ain't too worried about it. Fact is, those slaves did me a favor."

"A favor?"

"Yeah, got me a plan all worked out. I'm taking that stud in with me. I'm telling the sheriff I bought him last month, but part of the deal was I leave him here for a month for breeding."

"What about a title? He's going to want to see a title on that good of a horse. How are you going to be able to show him a title?"

Boddy smiled. "I'll write one up and sign it. You'll witness it and that'll be that."

The two rode back toward town leading the stallion. Once in town Boddy told the sheriff what they had found. A posse was formed in short order. Twenty-three men followed the sheriff and Boddy back to Red Oaks. Boddy had them excited, including the sheriff. They were ready for a hanging.

28

There would be no trial when they caught up with the escaping slaves.

When they reached Red Oaks, the sheriff sent men to check out each of the slave cabins. "We found one!" came a shout out of a cabin. "Hey, Sheriff, we found one, except she's dead."

"What? Dead?"

The sheriff reached the cabin and was met by one of the searchers. "Yep. Shot in the back."

The sheriff looked at the body and in a calm, unconcerned manner said, "Dig a hole and stick her in it. Then get yourselves up to the house." He started out the door, then turned back and said, "We've got white folks need to be buried."

The bodies were wrapped in sheets and three shallow graves were quickly dug. The sheriff used Donna Ann's bible and read a few verses.

"That's enough," Boddy said as he pulled the bible out of the sheriff's hand. "We can't spend all day here. We've got work to do."

"You are right, Mr. Boddy," the sheriff agreed. "I never had anything like this happen in this county before. Can't let those murdering devils get away. If they do, none of us are going to be safe in our sleep again."

The graves were quickly covered. No time was taken to mark any of the graves. They were leaving three people buried and no one would ever know who was in which grave.

The posse mounted and rode north. They came to the fork where Luke had sent Henry to the right.

"Well, Sheriff, which fork do we take?" one of the men asked.

The sheriff dismounted and walked down the left fork looking at the road.

"Half of us will ride to the right, the other half to the left."

29

He mounted up. "Let's go get 'em." He kicked his horse and started down the left fork. They had ridden less than half a mile when they heard a shot. Three more shots followed, one after the other. The sheriff pulled his horse up and turned around. There were three more shots.

"Let's go! They got 'em cornered."

The posse, ready for action, rode like there was to be no tomorrow. Back to the fork in the road to meet the rest of the posse. They rode up on the group standing in the road.

"Where are they?" the sheriff shouted.

"I don't know, Clyde, but I do know they are up ahead. Look at this," Boddy held up a cotton sack.

"What's that supposed to mean?"

"Look here," Boddy turned the sack over. Red Oaks was painted across the sack. "Old man Johnson put his mark on everything he had. I figured those shots would bring you back here and they did."

"Well, what are we waiting for? Let's get after 'em!" As the sheriff spoke, he mounted and started up the road.

It was four hours later when they found the empty wagon. The sheriff leaned over on his saddle horn and looked at Boddy.

"Well, Mr. Boddy, I suspect those slaves must have taken the trail I was on, wouldn't you suppose? We just gave them another full day's head start. We'll be lucky if we ever hear from them again."

Boddy's face showed his disappointment, but he did not offer an answer.

"I suppose, too, Mr. Boddy, I'll be wanting to take another look at those papers you had on Mr. Johnson's horse when we get back to town."

Chapter 4

"How much farther you think we have to go?" Luke asked Henry.

"Don't know for sure, but we have to be getting close." His voice trailed off as two men in uniform stepped onto the road from behind some brush. Both held rifles at the ready.

"Halt!" one of them shouted.

The wagon driver pulled up the mules. Luke stepped down from the lead mule and bowed his head. Slowly, he pulled his hat from his head and held it in both hands.

Four more men moved out of the brush. They had their rifles pointed toward the slaves.

"Where you bunch of people think you are going? You a bunch of runaways?" one of the men demanded.

"No, sir, we ain't no runaways. We are on our way to our master's brother's place. He has fields to put in. Master's brother took sick and his slaves are the ones that ran away.

Left master's brother with nobody to put in his crop." Luke did not look up as he spoke.

"Is that a fact? And what is your master's brother's name, boy?"

"His name is Master Tad Johnson, boss. He's the master of Five Oaks. My master is master of Red Oaks. His name is Master Harry Johnson. We haven't done any harm, boss. We're just field hands going to Master Johnson's to put in his crop and tend it 'til he can get him more slaves that don't run away when there is work to do."

"Hey, Corporal, I know that plantation, Five Oaks. It's about fifteen miles away over toward Dalton. These fools took the wrong road."

"Well, they can't get there from here without going back, can they?"

"Sure they can. About a mile up the road is a cut-through. Runs right to Dalton. It's not much of a road, but they can make it all right. This bunch of slaves ain't going to do harm to us. The Yankees got to be thirty miles on down the road. They can take that road and be in Dalton by tomorrow noon."

"Go on. Get back up on that mule and get yourselves out of here," the corporal ordered as he stepped clear of the road.

"Yes sir, boss, we'll be careful." Luke wanted to laugh out loud, but shuffled back to his mule and swung up on its bare back. "Let's go, you bunch of dumb folks. We got us a field to plant and we are wastin' daylight here." He kicked his mule and moved on down the road.

"Now, I'll bet you something, corporal. That black overseer is twice as tough on those slaves as any white one would be. Yes, sir, I just bet he leads them some kind of tough life."

Luke saw the lane up ahead and turned on it. The wagons followed. He dismounted and walked back and looked down the road. He lay down and crawled to a point just off the road. He watched. His wait was short. Two horses came out of the brush and headed back to where the soldiers were standing guard.

Luke smiled, "I thought they might follow us, just to be sure we were goin' to put in a field." He crawled back where he could not be seen and stood up. He dusted off his trousers. "OK, folks, we wait for about an hour then we get ourselves back on the road to the free line. We know it's only about thirty miles to the Yankees. Before we sit here any time I think it best if, Shorty, you and Buckeye get yourselves back down that road. Keep yourselves in the brush off the road and watch our back trail. If you see anybody comin', you high tail it back here and let us know. I think if you were to sit back there on that hill about a half a mile you could see that road a mighty long way."

Luke handed one of the young men a link of dry sausage.

"How long you want us to sit back there, Luke?"

"Here," he handed Shorty a watch.

"Where did you get this? This is the master's timepiece. I ain't gonna carry a dead man's timepiece. Not me. No, sir."

"This ain't the master's timepiece, you fool. This is mine. Edward gave this to me when he went away. Now you take it and when this little hand is on this number four, you get yourself back up here."

Shorty placed the watch to his ear and smiled, then put it in his front pocket.

The two boys were well out of hearing when Henry said, "I didn't know Master Edward gave you a timepiece."

Luke smiled. "He didn't. I found that one on the ground after we put the master in his bed back home. I just figured the master didn't have a need for it any more and maybe we might."

"You told those boys a lie. You said Master Edward gave

33

it to you."

"Well, what do you know? I did, didn't I? Guess I'll just confess when they get back." Luke chuckled. "Now, Henry, I have another part of my plan."

A puzzled look crossed Henry's face. He scratched his head. "You sure are doin' a lot of plannin' lately. Maybe some of us others might have a plan or two we want to do."

Luke saw the challenge for leadership and knew if they were to succeed, there could only be one leader. He had no intention of stepping down, not now that he had brought them this far. Especially not to someone like Henry.

"Henry," Luke said as he stood to his full height, "I'm about to tell you what I want you to do. Now, if you don't want to do it, that's somethin' else again. First, let me give you the plan, then you tell me what you think."

"Fair enough."

"Now, old Henry here," Luke put his arm on Henry's shoulder, "ran that third wagon up that blind road three days ago, then cut cross country and met up with us again. If we were followed from Red Oaks, chances are they followed that blind road and old Henry bought us some more time."

Henry's face showed signs of pride. Luke was giving him credit for the action he had taken. Luke knew Henry would be impressed with the recognition.

"Now," Luke continued, "I want old Henry to take one of these wagons and do the same thing 'cause he knows how it's supposed to be done. He'll light out up this road. You ee, those soldiers back yonder know we turned up this road. anyone comes up looking for us, they're sure to tell 'em we went this way. Ain't that right, Henry?"

"Sure is, Luke. My thoughts exactly."

Luke slapped Henry on the back. "Now, Henry is about to get that front wagon on down the trail. We'll leave some of our mess here like we did with that sack back yonder and if someone does follow us," he paused, "well, they'll think we ain't in no hurry. Fact is, we are, so you women and kids get yourselves in that second wagon and let's get rollin'. By the time we turn around, the boys will be back and we can get goin'."

Luke walked up to the wagon Henry was sitting in. He reached up. Henry took his hand and the two men shook.

"Old friend, when you get several miles up that road, cut the mules loose. You keep one for ridin' and head north. Maybe we'll meet up again. I hope so. If we don't, I'll always remember what you did to help us get out of this mess."

Henry smiled, showing his stained teeth. "Chances are, Luke, we'll be meetin' again in that freedom land." As he finished, he slapped the traces and spoke to his team, "Git, you flop eared son-of-a-guns. I don't want to see nothin' but bent ears and feel wind hitting me in the face."

Luke watched as the wagon turned around the bend and went out of sight.

The two boys who had been sent to watch the road returned and the one remaining wagon pulled back onto the main road. Luke and his people traveled until dark. They stopped to rest the team and ate another cold meal. The moon came up early and was almost full. With a moon lighting the way and being so close to freedom, they decided to move on up the road. With a short rest, the team would be ready to pull again.

Those in pursuit of the group had also decided to ride by moonlight in hopes of catching them before they were safe in the enemy's territory.

It was almost two o'clock in the morning when the posse was challenged by the Confederate road guard. "Hold on there," came the order from beside the road. "Who goes there?"

"Who are you?" Sheriff Davis demanded.

"The question is, who are you? Best make a statement or

else my men are going to blow you plumb back to wherever you came from."

"I'm Sheriff Clyde Davis from Pickens County. We are chasing a bunch of murdering runaways."

Three young soldiers stepped out of the brush. "Did you say sheriff? Why didn't you say so? We almost blew your heads off. We thought you were Yankee night riders, for sure."

"Well, we ain't. You see a bunch of darkies come by this way in the last day or so?"

"Yep."

"Well?"

"Well what, Sheriff?"

"Well, where did they go?"

"They were on their way to put in a field for their master's brother."

"That master wouldn't be named Johnson, would he?"

"Yep. That's what they said all right. Johnson from some kind of oaks. They said they were gonna put in the fields on some other oaks."

"Red Oaks? Did they say they were from Red Oaks?"

"Yep, that's what they said. Red Oaks. They were headed to Five Oaks to put in a field, so they said."

"How long ago did they pass?"

"Yesterday. Before noon."

"They go on up this road?"

"That they did. We followed 'em to about a mile yonder. Then they turned off on a little trail going west. That's the way to Five Oaks, don't you know?"

"You sure of that?"

"You doubting my word?"

The soldier drew back and moved his right hand to the trigger of his rifle.

"No, corporal, I'm not doubting your word. Can you

people show me that road? They're a bunch of cutthroats and we got to catch 'em. They killed a whole passel of white folks."

"Sure 'nuf, Sheriff, murderers like that need to be put in their place. A grave." He waved at a soldier standing next to a tree and said, "Private Turner, you show these fine lawmen where those slaves turned off this road."

The private disappeared for a couple of minutes, then out of the shadows he reappeared mounted. He rode to the center of the road about fifty yards away in the direction the wagons had gone.

"Follow him. He'll show you where they turned off. Followed 'em himself, he did, and saw 'em on their way."

The posse rode in silence to the cut-off.

"They turned down that old trail up yonder," Turner said as he pointed in the direction of the trail the wagons had turned on. "They aren't going to travel too fast on that old road. You can be sure of that."

"Much obliged, Corporal." As the sheriff spoke, he slapped the reins across his horse's neck and started after the young soldier who was already moving up the road. They reached the turnoff and rode for a few minutes, then stopped.

"Well, look at that, will you," the sheriff said. "Looks like they are sure they've got clean away. Stopped and had themselves a picnic right here in the middle of the road. Come on, boys, we are gonna have ourselves a hanging."

The sheriff struck his horse with his spurs and started off at a trot. "Yes, sir," he said, "the slave that can outsmart me hasn't been born yet."

Chapter 5

"Halt!" came the command as the group of exhausted escapees crossed a small wooden bridge. Luke pulled his mule up and raised both hands.

"Are you North or South?" he asked.

Three sentries approached with guns at the ready. The sentry did not answer Luke, but called out "Corporal of the Guards." Looking back at the group, he said, "You hold it right there, mister, until the corporal gets here and checks you people out."

The request for the Corporal of the Guards was repeated two times further down the road.

"Where are we?" Luke asked.

"Best you be still and don't make any move until the Corporal gets here."

The wait was short. Luke could hear hooves coming at a gallop. Four young men rode up in a cloud of dust. The

39

one out front moved closer as he asked, "What you got here, Private?"

"Got a wagonload of folks, Corporal, accompanied by three mules. I make out sixteen, maybe seventeen, counting young'ns."

The corporal looked at Luke. "You the leader of these people?"

"Sort of, I guess, but we ain't got no real leader." Luke had already decided he was in the hands of northern troops. Even though he was not aware of the politics involved, he knew the difference in the uniforms. As for politics, he knew that slavery was one of the problems and the North wanted to free the black man. The South wanted to retain slavery. Until now, Luke had no opinion. He had had a good job and until Overseer James went crazy, there were few problems at Red Oaks.

"What are you people doing out here this time of night? Don't you know there's a war going on? You could get these women and kids killed."

"Yes, sir, we know there's a war goin' on all right. We are runaways and we are on our way to the land of milk and honey." A big smile filled Luke's face.

"Milk and honey, is it? Well, let me tell you, you have got a long way to go. All you'll find around here is cold beans and maybe a cup of black coffee."

Luke slid down from his mule. "Well, sir, that's a mite better than we've had the last couple of days." Luke bowed his head as he shuffled his foot in the dirt. "We are in Yankee land, aren't we?"

The corporal laughed. "Yeah, you are in Yankee land all right."

"In that case, sir, I suppose I best tell you we got three guns in that wagon under them cotton sacks." The corporal tensed up and drew back. His hand fell to his sidearm.

"We don't mean to do any harm with them, but thought

40

I ought to tell you about 'em, so you know we are good slaves. We aren't troublemakers. We just want to be free."

"Private," the corporal ordered, "check out that wagon. You people in the wagon, get down on the ground and line up here. We are going to search everyone of you, so if you have any weapons, I would advise you to drop them on the ground." Several men had now surrounded Luke's group.

"Do what he says. You women folks, put your butcher knives on the ground." Luke bent down and from under his shirt produced Master Johnson's handgun. He laid it at his feet, then stepped back to the wagon and joined the others.

Once the corporal was satisfied that all the weapons were surrendered, he instructed the group to leave the wagon and mules and follow him. They walked in single file no more than half a mile when they came to an opening. Luke nor any of the others had ever seen so many tents. The corporal led the group to a tent where several lanterns burned.

"Now, you people follow me. Inside here, each one of you get a cup, a plate and a spoon. Then file by, one by one, and the cook will give you something to eat and a cup of coffee. When you get your food, go back to that opening over there," he pointed, "where those men are standing. You can spend the rest of the night there. Come morning, the colonel is going to want to talk to each one of you. Now, get yourselves something to eat."

"Thank you, sir," each said as they filed past the corporal. The corporal nodded to each who spoke. When all the slaves had their plates filled, they returned to the area the corporal had indicated.

"They sure are a motley crew, aren't they, Sergeant?" the corporal remarked to a man who had been standing just inside the tent. "I don't think any of them had on shoes, did they, Brown?"

"Don't believe more than a couple of the women did. To

tell the truth, Sergeant, I didn't notice much until after we got them in the cook's tent, but out of the lot there aren't five full grown men. Mostly women and children and half-grown boys.''

It was mid-morning when a young soldier approached the group. Luke watched as he came across the open area toward them.

"The colonel wants to see the leader," the soldier stated.

"Well, we don't have a leader," Luke said as he stood.

"Well, the colonel, he told me to bring him the leader and that's what I have to do, so I suggest you elect one and do it fast. The colonel doesn't like to be kept waiting."

One of the men stepped up to Luke and placed a hand on his shoulder. "This here's our leader." He looked at Luke with a degree of pride. "Fact is, you are our leader. You got us here and when it came time back there when Henry wanted to make some changes, you just took charge. Nobody here but you has done any talking ever since we started to run and look what we did. We got plumb away. That's what we did and you led us all the way."

Luke looked back at the young soldier who was showing signs of nervousness. "Do you mind if these two come with me?"

"I suppose it will be all right, if you can decide on a leader."

"Guess I'm it. You lead the way," he said as he started toward the tent area following the young soldier.

The colonel was a short, stocky man with a full beard. His eyes were as blue as the sky. His hair was unkempt and was covered with curls. He chewed on an unlit cigar. "Where are you people from?" he asked.

"We are from back there, master. From Master Johnson's Red Oaks," Luke answered. "Trouble is, we're ain't even sure where we are now, Master Soldier, sir."

42

The colonel smiled, then his face turned cold. His eyes narrowed. "Don't call me master." As quickly as his face had turned cold, it brightened again as the colonel pointed to his collar. "See this. This means I am an officer in the United States Army. I am what is called a colonel. Ever hear of a colonel?"

"Oh, sure, we had a Colonel Fry. He lived next to my old master's place. Everybody called him Colonel." Luke stared at the colonel's collar. "But he didn't wear nothing like that."

The colonel laughed. "Colonel Fry, you say. I'll bet the closest he ever came to being a colonel was a lump under his arm."

A young lieutenant standing behind the colonel laughed and added, "You're probably right, sir. Those southern colonels seem to come with almost every large plantation we run across."

The colonel nodded in agreement. "Now, boy," he said directing his voice toward Luke, "do you know what town you lived close to?"

"Oh, yes sir. It was Fairmount. Why it wasn't even a two day ride from our main house."

"Is that a fact now?"

"Yes, sir, it truly is."

"And why did you people run away? Can you tell me that?"

Luke looked down and half turned his body. He glanced up as he looked at the others. They were all afraid. None of them knew what to expect from these strangers. The rumor had been told that Yankees were the black man's friend. The North was the land of milk and honey. Now these questions and the tone of the colonel's voice put a fear into each one of them. Confused, lost and afraid they would be punished for a crime they did not commit, they were all filled with anxiety.

The colonel sensed their anxiety and moved quickly to dispense the emotion. "None of you have anything to fear here. You are safe. No matter what you did back there, nothing will affect your safety. Do you understand what I am saying?"

Luke looked up. "You mean no matter what happened, you ain't going to hang us?"

"Hang you? I give you my word. No one is going to hang you. Now what happened that made you run away?"

Luke told the whole story just as it had happened and why they decided to run away rather than be punished for the deaths of Johnson, his sister and the overseer. Luke told the colonel how he knew they would all be hung for a crime they did not commit.

"We meant no harm to come to nobody," Luke said, then added, "except maybe that overseer. I'm sorry about the master and I'm terrible sorry about Miss Donna Ann, but I have to tell you true, that overseer dying don't bother me one bit. And beside that, he done killed Mayla for no reason at all."

The colonel placed a hand on Luke's shoulder. "Don't fret about it, son. It's just one of those things. This whole world is stood up on its ear right now. We've got kin fighting and killing kin over this country of ours. This letting of blood has never been seen in this land before. You people have been so far removed from what is going on, I doubt if you could understand even a smidgen of it, even if I had the time to explain. I know you wouldn't understand, but some day you might. For now, let's just worry about today and leave tomorrow until tomorrow. As for what happened yesterday," he paused, took a breath, then added, "well, yesterday is gone forever. There can be no good come out of worrying about what happened, tragic as it had to be. What's done

44

is done.''

Luke could feel a new warmth in the colonel's voice. His fear had passed and somehow he felt he was in the presence of a trusted friend. He felt as safe as he did when Edward and he were alone back home. Other than Edward, he had never trusted a white man. Now somehow Luke knew the colonel was a trustworthy person. He could somehow feel it.

"Well, what are we to do with these people, Lieutenant Bowman?''

"Well, sir, we have been sending. . . .''

The lieutenant was cut off when the colonel raised his hand. His eyes were fixed on a guard bringing a single Negro man leading a mule toward them. The colonel spoke, his question directed toward Luke, even though he did not remove his eyes from the approaching pair.

"You know that man? Is he one of your group?''

Luke turned around. "Lord, yes. That's Henry. He laid a blind trail for us if we were followed. Besides, he's my mama's man. Yes, sir, boss, that's old Henry.''

"You mean he's your father?''

"No, sir. I mean he's my mama's man.''

For a second Luke's mind started to flash back to days gone by, but he quickly erased those thoughts. "Henry, you son of a gun. You OK?'' Luke called out.

A big grin crossed Henry's face, "Never better. Ain't nothin' wrong with me a few grits and a little hogback won't cure.'' He laughed as he finished his statement.

"Found this man back on the rim, Colonel. The sergeant thought you would want to talk to him. Seems he saw a bunch of Rebs back a ways.''

The colonel stroked his beard, "Is that a fact now? You want to tell me what you saw and where?''

"Mercy sakes, Master, I'd tell. . .''

The colonel interrupted, "Wait a minute. Are there any

45

more of your people scattered out there?'' he asked Luke.

''No, sir, this is the last one. We are all here now.''

''Good. Now I'm only going to tell you one more time, so all of you listen to me good. There isn't any more master. You are free men. So are those women and children over there. You don't have any master any more. Is that clear?''

Luke took a step and stood next to Henry as he spoke. ''This here's the Colonel, Henry. We don't call army people master. We call them by those little funny things on his collar. That's a colonel thingamajig. Ain't that right, Colonel, sir?''

''Almost. My name is Colonel Durks. Now, what about names? I want each one of you to give my lieutenant your name and he'll give you a letter. That letter will be your pass. I'm sending you all up to Richmond where you will be processed. From there, I don't know. Perhaps Baltimore. Luke, I want you to take Henry over to the mess tent and get him fed, then come straight to my tent. If this man saw some troops, I want to hear more about it. But right now he looks half starved. I'm afraid if we don't get him fed, he'll be thinking more about his stomach than what he saw.''

The colonel turned and left, followed by several others in uniform. Luke, Henry and the others followed the lieutenant back to where the other slaves were waiting. The lieutenant took the names of each slave and advised them to remain where they were until he returned.

Luke led Henry to the mess tent where he was fed. After Henry had eaten, Luke took him to the colonel's tent.

As they approached, a guard stopped them. ''Wait here,'' he ordered, then went inside the tent only to return a couple of minutes later. ''OK, come on in. The colonel will see you now.''

Luke and Henry went inside. Both men removed their hats and held them in their hands. The colonel and three other officers were bending over a map. The colonel looked up.

"You know what this is?"

The two men walked closer and studied the maps. The colonel watched them with renewed interest.

Henry placed a finger on the map then picked up his hand. "No, sir, don't make no sense to me. Just a picture of some kind. What about you, Luke? Can you make heads or tails out of this here picture?"

Luke nodded his head yes, then studying the map from another angle, he moved to one side. "Colonel, sir, this is the road I sent Henry on. This is like sittin' on a cloud and lookin' down on the countryside. Look here, Henry, this is where we ate the last of that sausage. Can't you see that? Why it's plain as day. The soldiers that stopped us was about here, I'd guess."

"Yeah, Luke, I does see it now. I sure does. Now ain't that somethin'? It is like sittin' on a cloud, ain't it?"

The colonel straightened up. He placed his hands on his hips. "Well now, gentlemen, do you suppose Henry here could show me where he saw those boys in gray?"

"You mean the soldiers from the South?" Henry asked.

"That's what I mean, Henry. Can you find the spot you saw them?"

Henry moved around the table on which the large maps lay. He studied the lines moving his fingers over the roads. He then followed a small creek. "Yes, sir, they were about here, I think." He studied some more, then moved again. The officers moved to give him room. "Yep," he said. "That's where they are, for sure. Got more tents there than I saw here. I saw them from a ridge I suppose would be about here." He pointed to a spot on the map. "More tents?" the colonel asked.

"Yes sir. Twice, maybe three times as many."

"Well, I'll be dipped in oil. So that's where they went. General Sherman's going to have a fit when he finds out they

47

slipped right through his lines." The colonel walked to the front of the tent. "Private!" he shouted.

"Yes, sir," came the reply.

"Get me a courier on the double."

"Yes, sir."

"Now, let me get a message written. You gentlemen," he waved his hand around the room to include Luke, Henry and the officers, "if you please." He went to his desk and sat down.

The officers saluted and directed the two Negroes to leave the tent with them. "Did I do right?" Henry asked.

One of the officers smiled and took Henry by his right hand. He shook it with vigor. "You did better than that, friend. You may have brought information to the colonel that could well bring this war to a speedy end. Yes, I would say you did very well indeed."

Luke and Henry went to the rest of the runaways who were sitting in a wagon waiting to be transported to wherever they were to be taken. Luke started to get up into the wagon when someone called his name. Luke turned around. Behind a wire fence was a young soldier. His once gallant uniform was now dirty and hung in tatters on his thin body.

"Luke!" he shouted again. "Don't you know me? It's Edward."

"Edward? Did you say Edward?" Luke started toward the prisoner.

"Well, bless my soul, it is you, Edward. Sakes alive, what's happened to you?"

"It's a long story, Luke, but this war is over for me. If I live out the month, I won't be fighting any more." He pulled back his coat and exposed a large dirty bandage covering his entire side. "Got me a load of grape. Lucky for me, none of it is rattling around inside of me." As he spoke, he became weak-kneed and almost fell. He kept from

48

falling by grabbing the wire fence.

"What are you doing here?" Edward asked as if the question just formed in his mind.

"That's a long story itself." Luke was wondering how he would explain to Edward what had happened back at Red Oaks. As he studied his problem, a voice called out from a guard tower.

"Hey, you! Get away from that fence. Want to get yourself killed or something?"

Luke looked up and saw a guard pointing a rifle right at him, taking aim. He held up his hand, "No, sir, not me. I was just talking to this here fellow."

"Well, get back with those other blacks before someone puts a hole in your sorry head."

"Yes, sir, I'm goin', I'm goin'."

"What happened at Red Oaks?" Edward pleaded.

Luke smiled. "I don't know what you're talking about, mister. You got me all mixed up with someone else. Must be your fever."

"You sorry nigger. You and all them others, you're runaways, aren't you?" Edward winked at Luke.

"No, sir, we are free. We got no reason to run. No, sir, we ain't running no more."

"Get over there now!" came a shout from the guard.

Luke started back to the wagon when he saw a horse being led up to the colonel's tent. His trained eye noticed something in the way the horse held his head. He walked over to the private who was holding the horse.

"My, ain't he a pretty one," Luke said as he patted the neck of the horse.

"This is the colonel's pride and joy," the young soldier said. "He thinks more of old Charger here than he does of his wife and kids."

"My, my, I can see why. This here is a fine animal. Too

49

bad about his leg though.''

"What leg? What are you talking about? There's nothing wrong with his leg. What leg are you talking about?'' The soldier stepped back and looked at each leg.

"This one here.'' As Luke spoke he picked up the left foreleg and rubbed the area around the ankle.

"Nothing wrong with that leg,'' the young soldier said.

"Oh yes, there is. See how he flinched when I rubbed it? I could tell it's hurting from the way he held his head when you was walking him.''

The colonel had come out of his tent and heard only a part of what Luke had said. He walked around and looked at what Luke was doing.

"What do you see, boy?'' he asked.

"This ankle. It needs some help, Colonel. If this fine animal was mine, I would wrap this leg fresh every day. I would keep him quiet for maybe a week and rub my special liniment in at least twice a day. Otherwise, this ol' boy is gonna be crippled up for sure.''

"How is it you know so much about horses?''

"That's always been my job. All I ever did was take care of Master Johnson's horses. Yes, sir, he had himself some real dandies, too. Nobody ever beat him in a race.''

The colonel stepped back and looked his horse over, then asked "You sure about this, are you?''

"Yes, sir, seen it before several times. It's like when you turn your ankle. It'll mend, but not if you stay on it.''

"Get me another mount, Private. Luke, you take Charger back to the stable area and fix him up.''

"I would, Colonel, sir, but I'm supposed to get on that wagon over there and go somewhere.''

"There has been a change. You go tell your people good-bye. You are to stay here with us. I'll give you a job as a civilian and you will be what is known as a mess boy. I'll

50

explain it to you later, but right now, all you have to do is take care of this horse.'' Luke thought about what the colonel said, then asked, ''You mean I belong to you now?''

''No, that's not what I mean. You belong to yourself. You work for me. Or I should say you work for the United States Army.''

''I work for the Army?''

The colonel shook his head in the affirmative.

Luke led the stallion over to the wagon. ''Nam,'' he said to his mother, ''I ain't going with you. You have Henry to watch after you. I have a job with the United States Army. I'm going to be taking care of the colonel's horse.''

''You mean you are staying here?''

Luke nodded his head, then answered, ''It's what I want to do. Maybe this is my chance to be somethin' besides dumb.''

Four soldiers rode up to the wagon. ''OK, you people, we've got to get this wagon out of here.'' One of the soldiers rode to the head of the wagon team, then called back, ''Forward.'' The wagon started to pull away from Luke.

Tears streamed down Namdbi's face. She sobbed and called back to Luke, ''Be careful, Luke. Remember me. Remember us all. Don't you ever forget.''

Luke put his right hand to his head, then to his heart. This was an old tribal sign she had not seen or used herself for many years. It meant, ''with all my brain and all my heart.'' She knew he would never forget.

Chapter 6

Just as Luke had predicted, the stallion's ankle was as good as new in a few days. This pleased the colonel in several ways. First, his favorite mount was once again ready to be ridden and, secondly, a major offensive was under way. Troops were being directed to the area and preparations were under way for a major thrust into what remained of the almost defeated Confederate Army.

Though the colonel would never admit to being superstitious, he would no doubt feel better riding the horse that had seen him through many a tight spot.

Since the beginning of the war, Colonel Durks' luck had kept him on an active front and in the middle of the war. He enjoyed every minute of the battles, the strategy of war and the excitement. It was the fact that he was fighting many of his old classmates from West Point that troubled him. The question had arisen more than once, "If I come up on one of my old friends in the heat of battle, will I be able to destroy him and take his life?'' Then as a response to his own question, he would answer, ''Until it happens, who knows what one will do? I only know I am right by standing with the Union and I will remain alive.''

A flash of lightening followed by the clap of thunder told everyone in camp that it was going to be a wet night.

''Luke,'' the colonel shouted.

''Yes, sir.''

''Get my mount inside the remains of that old barn. I want him healthy when we run through old Johnny Reb.''

''Yes, sir, Colonel. I'll keep old Charger dry if I've got to put a slicker over him, head to tail. Can you tell me somethin', Colonel?''

The colonel who had turned to go inside his tent stopped and turned to face Luke. ''If I can,'' he remarked.

''What's gonna happen to those fellows behind the wire fence?''

''Those prisoners, you mean?''

''Yes, sir. What happens to them now?''

''Well, to tell you the truth, Luke, I really don't know. Whatever does happen to them has to be better than what has happened to our boys at Andersonville.''

''Andersonville, sir?''

''That's a prison where a good many of our troops found themselves. To call it Hellsville would have been a more suitable name.'' He shook his head. His voice revealed the sounds of sorrow. ''Many a strong young lad went in there only to be starved to death or worse.''

''That same thing gonna happen to those fellows too?''

''I don't know, Luke, I really don't know. War is a terrible thing. It does strange things to the minds of some men. Perhaps. I suppose we could have holes for prisoners just like Andersonville. I would hope we didn't, but the gospel truth

54

is I don't know." A puzzled look came across the colonel's face as he asked, "Why do you ask such a question? Why should you care what happens to those men? They are the ones that have kept you and your people in bondage all these years."

Luke thought for a minute before he answered. He was trying to get his thoughts together so he would not be misunderstood. Yet at the same time, he did not want to chance doing anything that may bring harm to Edward. "Is there a reason?" the colonel asked again.

"No, sir, I guess not. I just wondered, because once a long time ago when I was but a pup myself, I was put in a cage. It was a chicken coop and I stayed there for almost a week. That's a bad way to treat a person, Colonel, sir. I just sort of wondered, that's all."

"Well, don't worry about it, son. Those people will get what they deserve. You can be sure of that."

Luke nodded, then said, "Best get old Charger in the barn before that sky opens up and pours a bucketful or two on us."

Once in the barn, Luke fed the stallion then rubbed his legs with his special liniment. As he worked he kept thinking about Edward. All the time Edward had been at Red Oaks, he had always been kind to Luke. There had been a sort of friendship between them. Never had Edward shouted at him or cursed him. Instead, Edward had shown an interest in Luke's work. He had, in fact, looked to Luke to teach him about the horses. This, of course, had pleased Luke and made him feel important, more than just a stable hand. A feeling he had not experienced too many times and never after Edward had left to go to war. Somehow there was a bond between the two young men. Luke felt closer to Edward than any other white person he had known. In fact, closer than anyone except old Ben and his mother, Namdbi.

What remained of the barn was small and the colonel's stallion was the only horse stabled there. Luke also used it as his place to sleep. The rain started, slowly at first, then it came in sheets. The wind blew with very hard gusts. Luke lit a lantern and hung it on a nail.

"What am I to do about Edward, horse? I can't just let them put him in a cage. If I try to let him go and get caught, I'd probably wind up in some cage right along side of him."

Luke sat down on a box and lost himself in thought, trying to figure out what he should do. He had just about worked out a plan when a voice from the dark called his name. He looked up, but did not see anyone. Then the voice was a little louder and he knew he was not imagining it.

"Luke," the voice called.

Luke walked to the place where the door had been. He peered out trying to see in the dark and through the downpour. A flash of lightening cleared the mystery. Standing next to the fence clasping the wire was a man. Luke staggered out into the rain shielding his eyes from the droplets. As he grew closer, he could see it was Edward. He clasped Edward's fingers on the wire.

"Edward, you'll catch your death out in this storm."

"Makes no difference, Luke. I'm a dead man anyway. When these Yankees get done with me, I'll be headed for the graveyard. Tell me, Luke, I've got to know what happened. Why are you here? Is my mother all right?" Luke hung his head and shook it.

"What happened?" Edward demanded.

"You wait here. I know what I have to do, Edward. Don't you move. I'll be back."

Luke turned and ran back to the barn. As he approached he saw someone standing inside with his back to the opening. "Lord have mercy, what am I going to do now? He's going to want to know why I was out in the rain. And if I help Edward, he's going to know that, too. Only one thing to do now." Luke reached down and picked up a rock.

56

He walked up slowly and heard the man say, "Just like one of those dummies to go roaming off in weather like this."

Luke brought the rock down hard on the man's head, sending him sprawling.

"Got to work fast," he said. He grabbed one of the tools he had used to trim the hooves on the colonel's horse and ran back to where Edward stood. He snipped the lower strand of wire.

"Get down and crawl under, Edward," he ordered. As he spoke, he pulled on the next strand to make more room for Edward to get through. Edward was out of the compound. Luke grabbed him by the arm and led him back to the barn. When they were inside, Luke rolled the soldier over. It was the private who had been on guard outside the colonel's tent. He had a blanket still tucked under his slicker.

"The colonel must have sent this over for me," Luke remarked.

"What happened to my mother?" Edward demanded.

"She's dead," Luke said as he stood up.

Edward grabbed Luke by the arm and spun him around. "What do you mean? She's dead?" Luke shook Edward's hand off his arm and stood his ground.

"Edward," he stated matter-of-factly, "I'm going to tell you what happened. It's the truth and to prove what I'm saying is the truth, I've put my life on the line to set you free. We don't have time to stand around jawing so just keep your mouth shut and listen." Edward was surprised at Luke's tone of voice, but did not challenge him as he spoke. Luke then told how overseer James had shot Master Johnson and how when Edward's mother was stopped she fell and hit her head. He stressed the fact that no one wanted to hurt his mother or his uncle. It was James that caused the whole thing to happen.

"That's the way it really happened, Edward. There wasn't

a slave in the group that wanted it to happen. It just did. If we would have stayed, you know good and well what would have happened to the lot of us. So we ran. I'm sorry your mama is dead, but I'm not a bit sorry I'm a free man. I didn't want your mama dead. Or the master either. It just happened and it was that overseer, James, who started it. He was drunk and he did it all."

Edward sank to his heels and squatted. He put his head in his hands and sobbed. "You don't have time for that now, Edward. You've got to get yourself out of here before this storm lets up or both of us are going to be back behind that wire."

"What am I going to do, Luke? There must be a thousand Yankees hereabouts."

"More like two thousand," Luke said, "but there won't be a problem if you do what I say. But you are in luck. Most everybody is going to be covered up while this storm is going on."

Luke reached down and took Edward by the arm. He helped him up. "Here's my supper." Luke handed Edward a rag with a biscuit and a chunk of dried meat tied up in it. "I want you to whack me on the head and tie me up." As he spoke he tied the private's hands and feet. "Then put some hay over me because it's got to look like I was already conked and tied when this fellow came in. Then you take his coat and hat. The colonel's horse here is as sound as any your uncle ever had at Red Oaks. Then you get yourself south. This war is just about over. That's what the colonel says and, believe me, he knows what he is talking about. So stay clear of both Union and Southern people. It wouldn't do any good if you got yourself shot now. Now that you are free again."

Luke turned around with his back to Edward. "What I told you about your mama was the truth, Edward. The fact that I'm putting my life in your hands should prove it."

58

Edward brought down a blow with a small pole. Luke sank to his knees, then fell forward. "God, I hope I didn't kill him," Edward remarked as he fell to his knees and held Luke's head. "God, don't let this man die, not because of me." He felt Luke's pulse in his neck, then looked up and under his breath said, "Thanks."

Edward did as Luke had said and covered him with hay. He then saddled the stallion and rode out into the night. The storm still raged and there was no problem, just as Luke had predicted. The guards, like those in the towers, were trying to protect themselves from the driving rainstorm.

It was after daylight when a guard found Luke and the private. When the colonel was advised, he ran through the mud toward the barn. He saw Luke sitting with his head bowed. Blood had crusted in his hair. "You all right, Luke?" the colonel asked.

"I'm OK, Colonel. But I'm afraid I've lost your horse."

"That horse is a small thing in comparison to a man's life. I can get me another horse. The main thing is you two aren't dead. I'm surprised that whoever did this didn't cut both of your throats."

"Suppose he was in too big a hurry, Colonel," Luke remarked.

The colonel agreed. "You're probably right. Lord knows I'd be if I were in his position. I'm afraid all his efforts were in vain, however. The South will never last out the month. Sergeant!" he shouted, "find out how those guards could let a prisoner of mine escape. I want the name of the one responsible for this and I want to explain a thing or two to that man."

The colonel walked to the old doorway. "I hate to lose old Charger like this. Especially to some Reb who will probably just ride back to his unit only to get himself and my horse killed."

Luke rubbed his sore head and thought, "He's not going to get shot, Colonel. Not Edward. He's going back to Red Oaks and wait this thing out."

Chapter 7

Three months had passed and the army was constantly on the move south, the last big battle lasting three days. No one slept much while the battle was raging. Now it was quiet again and Luke returned to his normal duties. He was grooming the colonel's new horse when a soldier came riding into camp. He rode straight to the colonel's tent and dismounted before the horse had fully stopped. Colonel Durks had heard the rider coming and stepped outside the flaps of his tent.

"Hold on there, soldier," he said as he half returned a salute.

"The war's over, Colonel!" the young rider gasped, trying to get his breath.

"The war's over?"

"Yes, sir. General Lee signed the paper yesterday. General Grant has sent dispatches to all command posts." As he spoke, he handed Colonel Durks the small leather pouch he had carried inside his shirt.

Colonel Durks opened the pouch and removed the contents. As he read, a smile appeared. He then threw his head back and shouted, "Hallelujah!"

"What does this mean, Colonel? I don't have a job any more?" Luke asked.

"I'm afraid so, son. I would say in a couple of months most of these men will be headed home."

A look of despair came across Luke's face. He had a job he liked and did well. He had a boss who was a fair and just man. The food was better than he had known before. Now it would all be gone. Once again his life was changing as quickly as one snaps his fingers.

"What am I to do, Colonel, if I don't have my job here with you?" For the first time, Colonel Durks realized that most freed Negroes like Luke would be lost and confused. With no skills except those related to agriculture, there were surely some hard times ahead.

"I don't know, Luke. I really don't know. I'll keep you on just as long as I can and maybe something will turn up. If it doesn't, I'll see about getting you a job back in my home state of Delaware. There are some good farms there and I'm sure there is always a need for a good hand somewhere."

Luke thought about what the colonel had said as the unit moved toward Richmond. The troops knew that once they reached Richmond, they were to be mustered out of the army. Most of the officers and the regulars would be reassigned, but all the blacks, like Luke, that had been hired on would be let go to do whatever they wanted to and go wherever they wished.

Orders were given and the unit was once again on the move.

"I'm not going back to a farm," Luke said half to himself,

half out loud. "I have combed my last boll of cotton and pulled my last ear of corn. If I can't get me a job with horses or something else like that. . . ." His voice trailed off. He was lost deep in thought and did not hear his name called. A tap on the shoulder caused him to jump with surprise.

A private Luke had talked to several times had walked up beside the wagon Luke was riding in. Luke had found himself a wagon with the tail gate down and climbed aboard. The private was carrying a stick and had his rifle slung over his shoulder. He had tapped Luke with his stick.

"You always sleep with your eyes open?" the private asked.

Luke gave a little chuckle and answered, "Naw. I was just thinkin' what a boy like me is going to do when I get to Richmond."

"If I was you, I wouldn't worry too much about that. I heard the colonel talking this morning and he said that he had a cousin who has a carriage shop or something close to Baltimore. He said something like he was going to try and get you a job with him, working on wagons and buggies."

"You heard him say that? He was gonna see about getting me a job?"

"That's what I heard. He was talking to Captain Greene. I think he's going to get you and old Billy Boy, the cook, both jobs there if he can."

Luke's whole outlook on life changed in the few minutes the two men visited.

"Well, I'll be. I suppose everything happens for the best," Luke responded.

"That's what they say, but I ain't too sure sometimes." Their conversation was cut short by the bark of a sergeant who shouted, "Swenson, get yourself back in ranks! You ain't out of this man's army yet and you still belong to me."

63

"Yes, sir, Sergeant Turner, but I'm mighty close to being cut loose, ain't I?"

The sergeant grumbled, "You bunch of people I have to put up with. Don't know how we ever won this war. The South must have really been messed up. That's all I can say."

Swenson returned to his place in the long column. Luke started to hum a tune. With the possibility of a job waiting for him, he felt better now than he had for several weeks.

The troops reached Richmond in the early afternoon. Luke went straight to Colonel Durks and took charge of his horse. About four o'clock, the colonel sent for Luke. When Luke arrived the colonel was signing some papers. Luke waited until Colonel Durks looked up before he spoke.

"You sent for me, Colonel?"

"Yes, I did." He folded the letter he had been writing and put it in an envelope. He sealed it and handed it to Luke.

"What's this, sir?"

"This is a letter to my cousin Harry. Harry Cotter. Harry is a man a little older than me. He has a company that builds wagons and buggies. I think you'll be able to find work with him." He handed Luke several bills. "This is your pay." He smiled. "It includes all your back pay, too. You have sixty-seven dollars there, Luke. That much money can take you just about anywhere you want to go and keep you fed for a long time, if you don't waste any of it."

Luke looked at the money in his hand, then placed it in his pocket. He slapped his free hand with the letter and said, "Where is Mr. Cotter at, Colonel? Because that's where I'm heading."

Colonel Durks smiled. "Good choice, Luke. You'll like Harry. He's just outside of Baltimore in a small town called Cockeysville. You just take the pike to Baltimore and when you get there you ask someone how to get to Cockeysville. When you see Harry, you give him that letter. I've told him

64

all about you. I'm sure he will put you to work."

Luke extended his hand. The colonel took it and stood up as the two men shook hands.

"You've been a good boss, Colonel. I'm a lucky man to have driven that wagon into your camp way back when."

"You're a good man, Luke. I'm sure I'll see you again some day, so I'm not going to say goodbye. I'm just saying take care of yourself."

"I'll do that all right, Colonel."

Luke gathered up his few belongings and started walking up the pike headed for Baltimore. The traffic was heavy and he caught a ride on a freight wagon. The driver charged him two dollars and promised a trip all the way to Fredericksburg. Outside of Fredericksburg, he caught another ride to Alexandria. From there he walked for three days. He spent the nights in wooded areas off the main road. He purchased what few supplies he needed from local farmers. Luke still did not feel right about going into places of business to make a purchase. North of Beltsville, he stopped at a farm house and asked if he could work for his supper.

"I'll cut you some stove wood, clean that barn out there, just about anything," he said to the farmer.

Elmo Warner was a man almost sixty years old and in bad health. He could use Luke's help, but times had been hard for him also. "Haven't got much to feed you, but I'll share what I do have," he replied.

Luke set about chopping and splitting the wood that was piled close to the house. Elmo brought out a pitcher of water and handed Luke a glass.

"Where you headed?" he asked.

"Got me a job up in Cockeysville," Luke answered. "Gonna work for my colonel's cousin building wagons."

"What do you mean, your colonel? Were you in the Army?"

65

"Oh, no sir. I just worked for the Army. Colonel Durks was my boss. When he had to let me go, he gave me this letter." Luke pulled the letter from his shirt pocket. "He told me to see his cousin who's got a business in Cockeysville."

"Building wagons, huh?"

"Yep. That's what he says all right. Building wagons."

"That cousin wouldn't be Harry Cotter, now would it?"

A surprised look came across Luke's face. "It would indeed. You know him, do you?"

"Know of him. Never met the man myself. I'm afraid I've got some bad news for you though."

"What kind of bad news?"

"I heard that place caught fire three or four months ago and Cotter was killed fighting the blaze."

"Killed? He can't do that. I need that job." Luke's voice was filled with disappointment.

"Tell you what. I'm needing some help around here. I can't pay much, but I sure can keep your old gut from growling and give you some pocket change, if you'll help me put in a crop."

"I do appreciate the offer, but I have to find out if Mr. Cotter's place really did burn and if he was killed in the fire. You said you just heard that. Maybe it was some other fellow what got killed."

"I can understand that. Besides, if what I heard wasn't true, you would sure enough have a better job than I can offer." The old man started back toward the house. He stopped and turned around. "Put that ax up and get yourself washed. I've got some fixin's on the stove. Let's eat before it turns dark."

Luke carried the ax down to the barn and laid it next to the other tools he saw in a lean-to shed attached to the side of the old building. He heard a horse whinny inside. He pulled open the door and looked inside. There in the stall was one of the most beautiful thoroughbred horses he had ever seen. He went in and patted the mare on the nose and looked her over. He opened the half door and went inside the stall.

"My, my, you are a beauty." He ran his hands down her foreleg. "Now, old gal, you got to be the best horse I have ever seen. I'll bet you can knock a hole right in the wind when you get to running at full speed." He patted the mare's neck as he left the stall.

Back at the house, Elmo had bowls set out and poured Luke a large glass of milk to go with his stew. The two men ate in silence.

When they were finished, Luke asked, "You live here alone?"

"Sure do. My wife passed on back in '61. Son got himself shot in the war. He's buried down close to Atlanta somewhere. Just me now. Thought about selling out and moving out West a time or two." He paused. "Truth is, I'm too old to start over. I wouldn't last through a winter out there. To think otherwise would just be foolishness on my part."

Elmo got up and went to the stove where he poured two cups of coffee. He reached up on a shelf and took down a jug. "You need yours sweetened some?"

"Think so," Luke responded.

The old man poured from the jug into the cups that were half filled with coffee. He crossed the room and set the cups down.

"There," he said, "that'll give you a new outlook on life." As he spoke he raised his cup to his lips and sipped. He let out a long sigh. "Now, that's prime stuff," he said as he smacked his lips.

Luke took a sip. The fluid burned his throat as he

swallowed. "That's plenty strong, that's for sure," he gasped. The old man laughed. "Yep. It is for sure. I'd say about as strong as you'll find in these parts. Made it myself."

They sat in silence drinking their spiked coffee.

After Elmo finished, he set his cup down. "Tell you what. You take a mule and ride up to Cockeysville and take a look see. If what I heard is true, you come on back and help me put in my crop. If it ain't true that they had a fire, you get my mule back to me first chance you get. Fair enough?"

Luke thought about it. He remembered how many people he had seen looking for work. He knew jobs were hard to find. "Fair enough, Mr. Warner, but you know I have to go see for myself."

"Sure do. Wouldn't feel right if you didn't."

"I have to ask you one thing for sure, Mr. Warner."

"What's that, Luke?"

"Where in the world did you come across a mare as fine as that one out there in the barn? That's got to be as good a runnin' horse as I've ever seen and, believe me, I've seen some good ones."

Warner made another trip to the jug, but this time he left out the coffee. He sat back down and sipped on his cup, then in a quiet voice he said, "That's my love out there. That Lady, she was going to make me rich. Would have too, if this war hadn't come along. Had a stud horse every bit as good, too. I was going to raise me a foal or two with 'em and race myself into riches. Right after the war started, someone stole my stud. Nearly stole Lady, too, but she, being only green broke, got away. After that, my boy went off and got himself killed. I just lost all interest in racing. What's an old fool like me need to be rich for anyhow? All I ever knew was how to put in a crop."

He emptied his cup and gasped, "That's truly good stuff. Should have sold Lady a year or two ago, but couldn't bring

68

myself to part with her. She's all I got left except for the land. I guess they'll bury us together some day." He laughed a dry chuckle. "Enough of that. I got to get to bed. Best you do the same. You can bunk down at the barn."

The next morning Luke started out with a sack of food Elmo had put together for him.

"You take care now, Luke. That's my best mule you got there."

"I'll take good care of old Sam, don't you worry." Due to bad directions or a misunderstanding, it was over a week before Luke reached Cockeysville. Elmo's information was right. There had been a fire and Harry Cotter had died fighting the blaze.

"Well, ol' mule, I guess you and me are going to put in a crop. Said I wasn't going to do any more farming, but that goes to show what I know. Suppose I just ought not say I'm not gonna, because every time I does, I do."

Luke spent the night in a wooded area outside of town and the next morning before sunup he was on his way back down the road headed for Elmo's farm.

Elmo was a gentle man and Luke found him an easy person to work for. The seeds were sown and the crop had sprouted. With good spring rains, there seemed to be no end to the weeds and Luke found himself from daylight to dark clearing the fields. Elmo would work right along with Luke for about half a day. The old man would be so tired out he would collapse under a shade tree and rest. Luke would help him up to the house and fix lunch. Then after a short rest, Luke would return to the field.

After supper, which Elmo always fixed, Luke would help him clean up. Then, after a couple of drinks from his jug, the old man would go to bed. As tired and used up as he was, come daylight he would return to his beloved field.

One day after taking a water break, the two men sat under

69

a tree. Elmo began to reminisce. "Luke, this old field has raised many a crop. My father cleared this field himself. It was back in '83, I think. Or was it '03? I can't remember any more. Doesn't matter anyway. He was just a young man then. He fought in the Revolutionary War. Saw the General himself one time, too. Yep, he told me he never saw anyone sit a horse like that man did. All full of pride and self-confidence. I always supposed it was General Washington. Now I think about it, I'm not sure who it was. He always just called him the General.

"When he got this farm, he and my mother got married and soon after, I came along. Like him, I only had one boy." He paused, took a deep breath, then continued, "That boy of mine, he would have worked this old field, too, if he had not been killed in that blamed war we just finished."

"What war was that your father was in?"

"The Revolutionary War. The one where we won our freedom from England."

"You mean your father was a slave, too?"

The old man chuckled. "No, not in the sense you are thinking, but I guess he was in a way."

"Well, don't that beat all. They have always had slaves here of one kind or another, I guess."

The old man smiled. "No. They haven't, Luke, and I can see right now I've got another job cut out for me."

"What kind of job would that be, Mr. Warner?"

"I'm going to give you some schooling. Before I'm through with you, you'll be reading and writing some, not to mention speaking with a bit more knowledge in the use of the English language. Yes, sir, Luke, you are going to learn to speak proper English. I may be a little forgetful, but I'm a good teacher." He paused. "Used to be one. A teacher, that is. In my younger days."

"You'll do that for me?"

70

"Starting tonight. Now, you had better get back to weeding and I'll head back to the house."

The rest of the afternoon as Luke went up one row and down another his mind toyed with the idea of being able to read and write. Speaking better did not move him too deeply, but to read, that was something he had always wanted to do. And now he was going to learn.

Chapter 8

Edward, once Luke had helped him escape, rode most of the night in the rain. Just before daylight, the rain slowed to a drizzle. The first creek he came to was flowing heavily. He knew he had to chance the crossing. If he made it, anyone following would be cut off, thus assuring his escape.

Charger blew and pranced. He did not want to take the plunge. He could sense the danger and balked. Edward reached up and snapped a limb from a low hanging branch. He pointed the proud horse toward the stream and gave him a kick with both heels. He shouted and at the same time whipped the horse's rump.

Charger plunged into the swift stream and was washed along with the current. His great strength overcame the current and slowly the opposite bank was reached. Edward had slipped off Charger's back and hung onto the downstream side of the saddle, his body floating free. Only his hands held tight to the saddle and mane. Clutched in his hand along with the mane was the bridle. Once the horse reached the far shore, Edward slipped back into the saddle. Charger had little trouble reaching the top of the low bank. Edward pushed the great horse on for several minutes until he was sure they were safe from the fast rising waters. He held his side. It ached, but he knew he could not give in to the pain. Slowly he pulled his shirt back. He was in luck. The wound had not opened up. He tucked his shirt back in and smiled.

"Well, old man, you've earned a rest, but we've got to move on before it is good light. Then you'll have all day to catch up on some rest and maybe I'll get rid of some of this hurt." As Edward spoke to his horse, he patted its neck. Charger seemed to understand and without hesitation he moved on down the dim trail.

Animal and man both were in need of rest when Edward pulled the saddle from Charger's back. He tied the reins to a bush that would permit the horse to graze. He placed the saddle next to a tree and prepared to stretch out and try to sleep. It was not until now that he noticed a small sack tied to the rear of the cantle board. He untied the strap holding the small bag and looked inside.

"I'll be," he said under his breath. He reached in and removed the contents. There were two small pieces of dried meat. "I forgot Luke saying something about his supper. This will hold me over until I can find a farmhouse or something."

He ate one piece and saved the second, although he was tempted to eat both. Until now he had not realized just how hungry he was. After he finished his meal, he opened his shirt and looked at his side. The bandage was dirty but dry.

"Thank God," he said, "the way that feels, I was sure it had opened up again." He rebuttoned his shirt and stretched out. Sleep did not elude him and he rested for several hours.

It was late afternoon when Edward was awakened by the sound of shouts and the cracking of a bullwhip. He moved to where Charger was staked and held the horse's nose to keep him from whinnying. Hidden in the oak mott, a traveler on the road would have a hard time seeing them. If Charger should whinny, those on the road would surely investigate. If this were the case, his escape could be doomed to failure, as he was sure he was still in an area controlled by the North.

There were three wagons in the small train led by a lone rider in front. They were not military, but it looked as if they were loaded with boxes of supplies bound for military use.

"If that's Yankee supplies, I sure ought to try to do something."

He looked around. He had nothing in the way of a weapon, not even a knife. "To help is one thing. To be stupid is something else," he thought. He watched as the wagons passed out of sight.

"Well, old horse, I guess you and me best think about moving on south pretty soon. Won't be more than two or three hours before dark and we'll be on our way again." He opened his small sack and took out his remaining chunk of meat. "I'll eat this and sometime tonight, maybe we'll find a house where I can get something else for tomorrow." His mind was racing as he planned his trip home. He was not sure where he was, but he knew he had to move south until he could find a landmark. A name, anything that would help him get his bearings.

During the night, he approached a small farmhouse. He waited in the dark, watching the house. He noticed that there was no livestock in the pen or nearby field. The moon had come up and he saw what he thought was a chicken house. The door was open and he knew the house was empty. "It's still too early for a garden, but maybe they've got a root

75

cellar." He tied Charger to a bush and crept closer. He saw what looked like the root cellar and slipped up to its door. He pushed it open slowly. The rusty hinges creaked.

He started in, when a match was struck and at the same time a woman's voice said, "Move one hair on your head and I'll blow you in two."

Edward froze. As he stood there, a lamp was lit.

"Now, turn around real slow like, so I can get a look at who's about to go into my root cellar," came the command in a clear, calm voice.

He turned slowly, his hands still over his head. When he turned around to face his captor, he saw a woman about thirty years old. She showed signs of the war in her face. Her dress was made from a cotton sack. "What are you doing here?" she asked.

"Looking for food," Edward answered.

"Ain't we all," she replied.

They stared at each other for a full minute.

Then Edward said, "Look, lady, either go ahead and shoot that scatter gun or put it down, because I don't have the strength to hold my arms up for much longer."

"You're a southern boy, ain't you?"

"Yes, ma'am. I am."

"Well, why in the blazes didn't you say so to start with?"

"To tell you the truth, I don't know where I am. I could still be in Yankee territory for all I know."

"Well, you ain't. You a runaway or something? You a deserter?" She raised the shotgun again.

"No, ma'am. I'm no deserter. I was a prisoner, but I managed to escape and I'm trying to get back to my company," Edward lied. The last thing he wanted to find was an army company of any kind. All he wanted to find was Red Oak and perhaps retreat to a life of peace and quiet. But now, even more than that, he wanted something to eat.

The pain in his stomach told him he was past his point of endurance. He became dizzy and sank to one knee.

The woman laid her shotgun down and helped Edward up. She assisted him inside the house and sat him in an old chair.

"When did you eat last?" she asked.

"Don't know for sure. Two, maybe three days ago," he answered.

"Well, you sit there. I'll get you something." She went to the stove and took off a pot. She poked at the ashes then added a few twigs. She placed the pot back over the open hole in the stove top. When the ingredients appeared to be warm, she poured a bowl full and set it in front of Edward. The smell made his mouth water.

Edward ate his stew in silence. After he finished, he asked, "What kind of meat was in the stew? It had a taste I've never tasted before."

"Opossum. You like it?"

Edward took a deep breath. "Well, I got him down. I'm sure going to try to keep him down."

The lady burst out in laughter. She stuck out her hand and said, "I'm Lorine Day and it's a pleasure to know you, Mr..."

"Lynn. Edward Lynn, ma'am, at your service." Edward stood and bowed like a southern gentleman.

"And where would you be heading, Mr. Lynn? I know you ain't lookin' for no army outfit. That is, unless you are plumb crazy."

"Back home to Red Oaks. I figure I've done my part in this war. Took a miniball in my leg a year ago, then got me some grape in my side. Spent a little time in a prison camp and now I'm going home. What about you? You live here all alone?"

"Do now. A bunch of Yankees came by about three months ago and killed my man. Ate my milk cow and all of my chickens. Since then, all I've had to eat is what I can scratch out of the ground and what few animals I have been able to kill. Got that opossum day before yesterday."

"That's all you got?" As Edward asked the question, he pointed toward the bowl.

"Yep. That's it until I kill me something else."

"You plan on staying here?"

"Guess so. It's home. Ain't got no place else to go."

"Why not come with me back to Red Oaks? There's plenty of room there."

She thought about the question for a minute, then answered. "Maybe. Why not? Nothin' left here worth stayin' for."

"How long have you been living here all by yourself?" Edward asked.

"Not too long. My husband went off to war and was gone about a year. He came home all shot up. When he came home, he was almost dead. I nursed him back best I could. He could hardly stand on his own feet when the Yankees came riding in and busted open the door and shot him while he lay in his bed. I was outside when they came so they never saw me or else I'd be dead, too. I knew I couldn't stop what was happening so I just stayed hidden until after they left. Then I buried John Paul out by those trees." She was now looking out the door into the dark. "Like I said, Mr. Lynn, I don't want you to misunderstand. I'm just a woman who is in bad need of some help. That's the only reason I would even think of going with you." She paused, "But I haven't said yes and I haven't said no."

With something in his stomach, Edward's strength had returned. He stood up and walked over to Lorine. He placed an arm around her shoulder. "Lorine Day, I understand exactly what you are saying. I haven't had all that much company myself as of late and, to tell the truth, I need a friend

78

and someone to talk to. Besides that, I need someone to help me and keep me from starving to death.''

Lorine looked up into Edward's eyes and could see that he was a sincere man, someone she could trust.

"Comes a time when a body's got to be truthful, even if it ain't the accepted thing to do," she said. "I know I can't stay on here alone, but I'll still have to think about it."

Chapter 9

When morning came, Edward awoke. It took him a moment to realize where he was. He sat up and listened. He strained to hear any sound, but there was silence. He slipped into his trousers and boots. As he went out the door leading to the old porch, he saw Lorine coming out of the trees. She had a rabbit hanging limp in her left hand. Slung across her shoulder by a strap was her shotgun.

She saw Edward standing in the doorway and held up the rabbit. "Breakfast," she called out.

"I never heard you shoot."

"Shoot? My goodness, man, I ain't going to waste a shell on no rabbit. Haven't got that many to go wasting them, not on any rabbit anyway."

"If you didn't shoot him, how did you get him then?"

She chuckled, then answered, "Snares. I have about thirty of them set out there in the woods. That's how I caught that old 'possum you ate last night. When you rode in, you broke about a half dozen of them yourself.''

Lorine cooked the rabbit over an open fire in what was left of the fireplace. After they had eaten, she and Edward passed the time with small talk.

"Well?" Edward asked.

"Well what?"

"You going with me to Red Oaks?"

"Maybe. Ain't really made up my mind yet. You married?"

"Nope."

"You got someone there? A girl you might be interested in. Someone like that?"

"Nope. From what I heard I don't have anybody. Word came to me that all my folks have been killed."

"Then what are you goin' back for?"

He thought for a moment, then answered, "Got to see for myself, I guess."

Lorine nodded. "Guess you would never feel right if you didn't. Yeah, I'll go with you, but nobody's goin' anywhere for a few days. Your side needs some doctorin' and besides that when I was out I could see a lot of troops moving on the road over yonder." She tossed her head in the direction of the woods.

"You saw the road?"

"Yes. About a mile or two away." She pointed as she spoke. "Up on that hill there is a point. I always watch the road when I'm out there. Never know what is going to come down it any more."

She sat back down at the table. "I figure we should wait for a couple of days. That will give you a chance to heal up some and we will be less likely to run into anybody. Maybe they'll all be gone by then. The troops, I mean."

Almost a week passed before they started on their travel

82

toward Red Oaks.

"When you see the main house, you will lose your breath," Edward told Lorine. "There are six large columns across the front veranda."

"I'll bet there is a huge tree sitting right close to the house, too," she answered.

"As a matter of fact, two of them," Edward laughed. "Yep, I just can't wait to see your face when you see that house." Edward smiled. He really was pleased to be going home and even more pleased Lorine had decided to accompany him to Red Oaks.

When they reached Red Oaks, Edward could not believe his eyes as he stood across the field and looked at the remains of the once grand mansion.

"My God, what do you supposed happened?" Lorine asked.

Edward's disappointment was written across his face. Tears welled up in his tired eyes as he pondered the question. Then shaking his head, he said, "I have no idea. Luke didn't say a word about this. He must not have known or surely he would have told me that there was a fire."

"Who is Luke?"

Edward shook his head as he spoke, "A man I know. Doesn't matter. Let's go on into town. Can't stay out here. Not now."

He pulled himself up onto the saddle and reached a hand down for Lorine and helped her up behind him.

They had ridden no more than three miles when Edward saw a wagon coming toward them on the road. As the traveler came close, he recognized the wagon driver.

He called out. "Morning, Mr. Lambert.

The driver pulled up his team. "Who is that?" he asked, straining to see who was speaking to him.

"It's me, Mr. Lambert. Edward. Edward Lynn."

"Edward Lynn? Old man Johnson's Edward Lynn? Well, I'll be doggoned to blazes and back. We were all told you were dead."

Edward smiled. "Well, thought I was myself a couple of times, but here I am."

"You been out to Red Oaks?"

"Yes, sir. How did that happen? I mean how did it catch fire?"

"Yankees put the torch to it, they did. You know about your folks being killed by the slaves your uncle had working the place?"

"Know about them dying? Yes, sir, I ran into Luke. He told me the whole story. He says it was the overseer who killed my uncle. Then they killed the overseer. My mother was killed by a fall when they tried to settle her down. Then knowing full well that they would be blamed, they lit out. Can't say I wouldn't have done the same if I were in their place."

"Hmmm," the old man said as he ran his finger through his thick mop of gray hair. "That makes more sense than that cockamamie story Boddy told."

The old man reached behind the seat and picked up a jug. He pulled the cork from the top and took a long drink. He then handed the jug to Edward.

"Best take a good pull on this, boy, before I tell you another piece of bad news."

Edward took a long drink. The fluid burned as it went down, but tasted good. He handed the jug to Lorine. She took a small sip and passed it back to Edward.

"Well, what's the bad news?" he asked.

"You ain't got Red Oaks no more, son. It was sold last month to some people from up north for the back taxes. Ain't no use trying to fight it either. Some have and all of 'em lost. If I was you, I would just strike a trail out west and start all over again. They say there is gold for the finding

84

in California. That's where I'd head for if I was you."

"You sure there is no chance to get Red Oaks back, Mr. Lambert?"

"I'm sure, boy. No more chance than a snowball in July. No chance at all."

Edward turned half way around and looked at Lorine. "Want to go to California?"

"Why not?" she replied.

"I'll be thanking you, Mr. Lambert. My friend and I may just take your advice and go to California."

The old man tipped his hat and popped his team with the reins. Edward and Lorine watched as he drove down the road and around a bend.

They rode back to Red Oaks. Edward poked around the ashes looking for something, then he bent down and removed what had been part of the fireplace hearth. He took out a small metal box. Then slowly, he opened it.

"My uncle always kept a little cash hidden here," he said as he opened a small sack that was inside the box. He poured several gold coins out onto the palm of his hand. "Looks like a little over two hundred dollars." He took the coins and put them in his pocket, then picked up the paper money. The heat had scorched it, but it was still readable. "This isn't worth much. All of it has Jeff Davis' picture on it. We'll just leave it for someone else to find." He returned the box to its hiding place and kicked ashes over the spot.

"We've got two hundred dollars, one horse that is about half lame and a long way to go. First chance we get we'll get us a couple of good horses and a sack of food. Then we'll be on our way."

"Well, we ain't got no reason to hang around here," Lorine said. "Let's get goin'."

"Wish I would have said that," Edward remarked as he helped her up behind him. "You should have seen this place like it used to be. There was not a grander house in these parts, I promise you.''

Chapter 10

Luke put in the crop and worked it throughout the growing season. Then almost single-handedly, he harvested Elmo's crop.

"Well, Mr. Elmo, I think we just about did what we set out to do. You've got a crop and I can read and write a little. With some practice and those books you gave me, I might even write you a letter one of these days."

Elmo looked up. "You planning on leaving, are you?"

"Yep. I hear that the government started a new thing in the Army about a year ago. They've got some regiments of black soldiers now."

"You thinking about joining up in the Army? I would have thought you saw enough of that when you worked for them."

"A man in town told me they pay thirteen dollars a month, give you a suit of blue and feed you three squares a day. I think I'll just try that for a while, especially if I can get in a horse outfit.''

The old man thought about Luke's statement a long time before he reacted, then he said, ''You know where to sign up? I mean, you don't just sign up any old place, you know.''

''Yes, sir. I've got to get myself to a town called Greenville. It's down in Louisiana, I was told.''

''How you gonna get there? Fly?''

Luke smiled and cast his eyes down at his empty plate. ''No, sir. Thought I would ride the train part way, maybe walk or catch a ride on a freight wagon the rest of the way.''

''Train tickets cost money. You haven't got any of that, have you?''

''You know I don't have any money left. Spent what I had on some of that seed we put in last spring. Kind of felt since I paid for some of the seed and did most of the work, you might give me the price of my ticket.''

''You know I don't have any money. Not until I sell some of that grain anyway. I couldn't give you anything right now. How much is a ticket to this Greenville place anyhow?''

''Best I can find out, about thirty-five dollars will get me all the way. That includes one meal a day.''

The old man stood up and walked to the window. He looked out toward the field. The shadows were growing long and in the fading sunlight, he reminisced about his younger days. After several minutes, he turned back to face Luke who was still sitting at the table. ''I need you here, Luke. I truly do. By the same token, you need to do what you've got to do. Tell you what, tomorrow you take a wagon into town and sell a load of that corn we have out there in the barn. Whatever you get for that load will be yours to keep. If it's less than the train fare, you'll just have to make it do. If it's more, you'll have some rattling money to carry along. That sound fair to you?''

Luke's entire face lit up. His smile showed his approval

even before he spoke. "Fair enough, Mr. Elmo. You've been a good boss and I'm beholden to you for helping me with my learning. I truly am."

He offered his hand. Elmo took it and they shook to seal the bargain.

Luke delivered the load of corn to town and sold it to a buyer for the government. When he returned, he showed Elmo the money.

"Got me thirty-nine dollars," he said. "I'll be leaving in the morning. Think you could drive me back into town to the train station?"

"Nope. I really don't think I can. Tell you what I can do, however. You take old Bertha and leave her at John Upper's stable and I'll pick her up next trip I make into town."

"I'm obliged to you, Mr. Elmo."

Luke arrived at the depot early the next morning and purchased his ticket. He was told he would have a four hour wait for his train to arrive.

He paced the dock, straining his hearing and listening for the sound of the whistle. He had been told that the engineer always blew it about a half mile out of town. After almost two hours, Luke walked back to the ticket agent and asked, "That train, sir, you reckon it'll be on time?"

The old man working behind the window looked up. He had been watching Luke. He could tell Luke was anxious and a little nervous. "You on your way to get married or something, are you?"

Luke felt a rush come over him. He felt embarrassed and hung his head. "Naw, I'm not going to get married." The tone of his voice gave him away and showed his embarrassment.

The ticket agent picked up on it and enjoying the position he had put Luke in, he asked, "Well, what is it then? Your wife expecting a baby and you are trying to get home before that young'un gets here?"

"Heck no," Luke responded. "I don't have a wife. I'm going to join the Army."

"Join the Army?"

"Yes, sir, I truly am. I'm going to join the Army."

"Well, bless my soul. I suppose if you are going to join the Army, I owe you the truth. That old number 12 is on time most of the time." He paused. "But then again, she has been known to be a bit late. Just last month, she came in here almost six hours late." He paused again and rubbed his chin. "Then about a year ago she ran almost two days late." He saw the anxiety in Luke's face. "But today," he added, "I was told by the telegraph fellow over there," he made a motion with his thumb over his shoulder, "she's on time. Should be here in about two hours." He chuckled then added, "Don't worry about it. You are going to have yourself a long ride when she does arrive."

Luke thanked the old man and walked to the end of the dock and sat down. The two hours turned in to almost three before Luke heard the whistle. He watched and a feeling of excitement built up inside him when he saw the big black engine come around the curve.

After Luke boarded, he had another hour and a half wait before he felt the cars give a jerk and start to roll. He had selected a seat in the second car from the rear of the train. The conductor came in and looked over the passengers. He walked straight to Luke's seat.

"You have a ticket?" he demanded.

"Yes, sir, I do." Luke showed his ticket.

"Well, you can't sit here. You'll have to ride in the baggage car along with the porters."

The conductor turned and started back down the aisle. He stopped and turned. Luke, still sitting in his seat, was somewhat confused. He had paid full fare. He was a freed

90

man and, from what he had been led to believe, the people in the North felt different than those in the South about blacks. "Well, what are you waiting for, boy? Come with me. I'll show you where your kind ride."

Luke slowly rose to his feet and followed behind the conductor. He was taken to a baggage car. There was a bench against a wall. There were no windows, except three very small ones. They were high and had bars on them. Freight was stacked from one end of the car to the other. There was a narrow aisle that allowed passage on one side. That was where the wooden bench he was to use was located.

"I paid good money for my ticket. I don't understand why I have to ride here and not in one of the chair cars like everyone else."

"Look, boy, I don't make the rules. I only enforce them. This is where you ride or you don't ride at all. Now suit yourself."

Luke had not noticed the old black man sitting in the corner until the conductor had left.

"Best just set yourself down, son, and enjoy the ride. You ain't gonna get nowhere but throwed off if you get in an argument with that conductor. He ain't too high on us black folks. To tell the truth, I've been treated better by some southern people than some of these northern ones."

Luke sat next to the old man. The old man's uniform was neat in appearance. The brass buttons sparkled from being polished. Luke read what was written on his cap. "Porter. What's a porter do besides ride in a freight car?" he asked.

"Well, I do what the white folks don't want to do," he chuckled.

"Like what?"

"Like load and unload. Clean up. What needs to be done, I do it. Ain't bad work. When we're moving, I just sit back and enjoy myself a train ride. Hell, boy, lots of white folks

91

ain't never rode on a train. You know that? Now and again that boss of a conductor will have me do some chore, like help him with some old person or clean up a mess someone left behind."

Luke sat down beside the porter.

"My name's Hank," the older man said as he extended his hand.

Luke smiled and clasped the hand being offered. "Mine's Luke. You been doing this a long time?"

"A couple of years now, maybe a little longer. Mighty lucky to have a job like this, too. What do you do?"

"Been farming, but now I'm on my way to join the Army."

The old man burst out laughing. When he caught his breath, he gasped for air between words, "Join...the... army? My word, boy, ain't you heard they let all the blacks they had in the Army go when the war was over?"

"No, sir, didn't hear that. Seems funny they would be hiring others, but they are starting up some black troops. Gonna go out west I heard."

"Is that a fact?"

"Sure is. Going out to fight the Indians and open up the travel so it will be safe for folks to go all the way out to California."

The old man took off his cap and scratched his head, "California, huh?"

"Yep, and I'm going to be part of the ones who do it."

Hank went to the far side of the car and lit a small coal-oil stove and put a pot of water over the flame. "Bet you could stand a little coffee, couldn't you?"

"Bet I could," Luke answered.

Hank came back and sat down, "Now, you take those passengers back in the chair car. If they want coffee, they are plumb out of luck. They have to wait until late this afternoon when we stop before they get a chance to get some." He chuckled. "Riding here we get ourselves coffee any time we want it. Some things ain't as bad as they seem, boy. It's all in how the seer sees it."

Luke thought about what the old man had said and how it applied to him now that he was free. He felt he had paid good hard-earned cash for his ticket, the same as everyone in the chair car; but because he was black, he was not permitted to ride with the others. The old feelings were still there, and his liking or disliking the situation was not going to change a thing. His mood began to change almost as if magic was being worked. He began to wonder about his new life, the life of a soldier. Not just a soldier, but a cavalryman. A horse soldier. He remembered how the young men in the infantry used to talk about the cavalry when he worked for Colonel Durks.

"Lordy, lordy, Hank, I'm gonna be in a unit that rides all over the West, once I'm in that Army."

The old man shook his head, then remarked, "Heard tell the Indians ain't nobody to mess with. They can be plenty tough. You have to remember, you'll be in their back yard now. It isn't going to be like stealing chickens out of your old master's hen house. No, sir, those folks don't cotton to strange people, so I've been told."

"What have you heard about the Indians?" Luke asked.

"I've heard travelers talk now for over two years while I've worked for the railroad. Worked in the yards for a while. Yes, sir, I may be old, but I ain't deaf. I heard one fellow say the Indians can skin a man and keep him alive a week if they want to."

Luke laughed, "That's nothing but talk and you know it. Nobody can skin a man and then keep him alive a week."

"Maybe so, but the fellow I heard tell about it said that's what they did to his friend. That's all I know."

93

The rest of the trip Luke and Hank had very little to talk about. Hank had his work to do and Luke sat thinking about what the old man had said. Could Indians really do that to a man? The question seemed to have no answer.

Hank had left the car and been gone most of the day. When he returned, he brought in a small sack. "Well, I got you some vittles here, boy. You'll be getting off the train in about an hour or so, if we don't lose our steam. Tonight you'll probably be wishing you were back on this old train and having her rock you to sleep again." He chuckled.

Luke took the sack and thanked the old man. He then crossed the car and looked at the landscape through a crack in the wall. The trees seemed to be different. The lush green made him feel good. He felt like he did when he first left Elmo Warner's farm. The adventure had caught him again.

The train pulled to a stop and the large side door was opened. Luke looked outside. There were several people standing around as if waiting for someone.

"This is the end of the line," Hank said. "This is.where you get off. You make your connection here, boy, for the rest of your trip."

Luke thanked the old man for his kindness. He picked up his bedroll and jumped to the ground. Luke asked a middle-aged man standing on the platform where he could catch his next train.

"Well, they told me yesterday it would be in about 4:30, but here it is almost 7:00 and she ain't here yet." He pointed toward an office with its door open and added, "Might ask in there. That's where the station master has his office."

Luke thanked the gentleman and approached the open door. Inside sat a fat, older man with almost no hair on his head. He wore tiny round glasses. The glasses were much too small for his round face and when he looked up, Luke almost burst out laughing.

"What do you want?" was the way he greeted Luke.

Luke looked over his shoulder to see if someone was behind him.

"I'm talking to you," the fat man said in a very disrespectful manner. Luke felt his face get hot and his ears felt as if they were on fire. The rage he felt was building fast. After being forced to ride in the freight car and paying the same price as the chair-car passengers, he had just about had all of this type of treatment he was going to stand for. Luke stepped inside the office door and closed it behind him.

"I'll tell you what I want."

"What are you doing? Open that door!" the man demanded in a quiet voice that showed nervousness.

"When I leave, I'll open the door, but until then, I think it's time some of you people start remembering what a bunch of northern boys died for. Perhaps no one told you yet that we black people are free. We are Americans, too, now. So don't go shoutin' at me, mister, because I may just shout back. From the looks of that body you got there, I'd say you couldn't stand too much of my shouting. Now, why don't you say it right? Let me get you started. May I help you? That's how you do it. Watch my lips and I'll do it one more time real slow. May I help you?"

The fat man swallowed. Sweat had broken out on his forehead and started to run down his face. "I'll. . .I'll call the law," he stammered.

"No need to do that." Luke's voice was very calm and he repeated himself very slowly, "May I help you?"

The fat man wiped his face with a handkerchief, then said, "May I help you?" His voice was weak and broke like a teenager whose voice is changing.

In a very business-like manner, Luke responded, "Yes, sir, Mr. Station Master, you surely can. I am ticketed for the 911. I understand it is going to be late. Could you by any chance be so kind as tell me when I could expect that train to arrive?''

The fat man swallowed again. "Yes, sir," he said, "around ten tonight. They had some track problems, but we received a wire just a little while ago. It's all been repaired and the 911 is rolling right now."

Luke smiled. "See how nice it is when we understand each other. I don't mind waiting now that you've told me what I needed to know. I thank you, sir." Luke turned and walked out of the office. He closed the door behind him.

It was almost eleven o'clock before the 911 rolled into the station. Luke kept watching for a sheriff or deputy. He felt the fat man surely would cause some trouble, but to his surprise none came.

"All Aboard!" came the call and Luke boarded the train with his ticket in his hand.

"Where do we ride?" he asked a porter. There was no use in going through what he had already decided could not be changed.

"Third car up front," came the reply from the porter. Luke found the freight car. It was much like the first one he had ridden. He curled up in a corner and went to sleep.

The next day while the train stopped at a small town, Luke walked to a store and purchased himself a chunk of cheese and a bag of soda crackers. Luke spotted a can of peaches. "Now that truly would go good with my supper tonight." He added the can to his supplies. He went back to the train. A porter about his age was standing next to the open door of the freight car. "Howdy," Luke said as he started to reboard the train.

"I was told by Porter Jim you are on your way to join the Army. Would that be true?" the young man inquired.

Luke felt a spark of pride swell in him as he said, "That would be true all right. Gonna be a horse soldier."

"My, my, we have come a long way in a short time, haven't we."

"We have indeed," Luke answered, "but nowhere near where we have to go."

The young man laughed and started walking off. He looked back and said, "I know what you mean, but that day is comin'. Sure is."

Luke entered the car and cut himself a chunk of cheese. It was almost two hours before they were on their way again.

For the rest of the trip, Luke saw the old porter named Jim from time to time, but other than him, no one entered the car. It was early in the morning when they pulled into New Orleans. Luke had been told it was just a short distance to the little town of Greenville. He gathered up his few belongings and slid the door open and jumped to the ground. He looked around and saw an old lady. Tipping his hat he asked, "Ma'am, which way is Greenville?"

"Just follow this road that way," she pointed in the direction of Greenville.

Just out of the main part of town, a passing freighter offered Luke a ride all the way to Greenville.

Once he had reached Greenville, he started walking toward what he felt was the center of town. He had gone only a couple of blocks when he saw a soldier. To his joy, it was a black soldier. Luke could see he was a sergeant. He walked up and introduced himself.

"Morning, Sergeant. My name's Luke and I would be looking for the place where I sign up to be a horse soldier."

Cold eyes looked Luke over. Not an expression could be seen. Luke felt a chill come over him.

In a voice that was as deep as thunder, the sergeant responded, "Well, bless my soul. What makes you think we want a boy like you in our ranks?"

Luke's eyes turned cold and his anger built up to a point

where he felt he would explode. He had been talked to all of his life as if he were nothing, but since working for Colonel Durks, he had not stood for any abuse. He tightened his grip around the rope on his bedroll. He remembered watching how some of the privates had worked sergeants when he worked for Colonel Durks.

"Well, Sergeant, I worked for Colonel Durks during the war. I'm part man, part horse, and I can whip just about seven of anything that crosses my path if I take a mind to. Since this is a fighting man's army, I know you want only the best. I'm the best you've ever seen, too."

The sergeant stared, then broke into a smile showing his white teeth. "I'll just bet you are, too. Or at least, I can make you one of the best. Come with me, boy. I'll get you signed up in no time and we'll see just how tough you are after a week or two of old sarge looking after you."

The recruiting office was another three blocks away. As the two men walked, the sergeant asked several questions. Luke gave him straight answers. When the lieutenant swore Luke in, he asked, "Can you sign your name?"

"Yes, sir, I sure can. I can also read," he answered, then added, "some."

"Is that a fact?"

"Yes, sir, I surely can."

"Then read this for me." The lieutenant handed Luke a sheet of paper.

Luke studied it for a minute, then read what was written on it.

The lieutenant looked at the sergeant and said, "Well, Sergeant White, it looks like you've got yourself a corporal to help you with your paper work."

"Yes, sir, it does look that way."

"We have just a slight problem here, don't we, Sergeant?"

"How's that, Lieutenant, sir?"

"We have a man named Luke, but what about a last name?" The sergeant picked up the sheet of paper in front of the lieutenant and glanced over it, then laid it back down.

"What is your last name, boy? You do have a last name, don't you?"

Luke picked up the paper and chuckled, then said, "Suppose I was so glad to be signing up in the Army, I just plain overlooked that part, Sergeant."

Luke's mind was racing. He had not even thought about a last name. Up to now, it had not been necessary. Now he had to come up with one fast. He glanced out the window. As he did, a rider went by on a big gray Tennessee walking horse. His old master, Johnson, had had one almost like it. Luke had always liked that old horse. He looked back at the lieutenant, "Gray, sir, my last name is Gray."

"Well, Corporal Gray, Sergeant White here will get you the things you need and get you started on your new career right away."

Luke made an effort to salute. As clumsy as it was, the lieutenant returned the courtesy. "By the way, Corporal," the lieutenant added, "you'll be getting fifteen dollars a month."

"Yes, sir. But, Lieutenant, I thought it would be thirteen. Did I understand you to say fifteen?" Luke said. He felt he would burst with pride. He had never expected to make that much money.

"Privates get thirteen. Corporals get fifteen," the lieutenant said as he turned back to his paperwork.

Sergeant White led Luke to a tent where several men were sitting on boxes outside. They were working on saddles.

"This will be your quarters. We've got plenty of work to do before we get started with our training, so you work with these men and get these saddles soaped. When you've finished," he paused, then added, "we'll find something else.

Just about every one of these saddles need new girths or leather replaced somewhere on them.''

Luke nodded and pitched his bedroll inside the tent, then sat down on the end of a box.

"Looks like every one of these needs something fixed on it," he said.

One of the soldiers laughed, then said, "Sure do. If we want to ride in 'em we got to fix 'em up. If you'll just look over there, you'll find yourself one to work on.'' The soldier pointed to a tent next to the one they were sitting in front of. "After we have fixed them, we soap them. The sergeant, he wants them like new when we finish.'' Luke went to the tent and looked inside. He saw more saddles than he had ever seen in any one place. He picked one up and returned to his place. He started to work on the broken girth.

"Where did all those saddles come from?"

"Beats me. They came in a couple of days ago and Sergeant White said we got to fix them. Looks like we got every saddle ever ridden during the whole war, doesn't it?''

The rest of the week the men worked on the tack, saddles, bridles and halters. Four big wagons were pulled in and loaded with the items the men had repaired.

It was midway into the second week when Sergeant White told the men they were going to start their training, but would move to another area. They rode for the biggest part of the day in back of a wagon. Their number had now grown to more than fifty.

As the wagon pulled into the compound, Luke sat taking in the entire layout of the camp. He could tell it was much like several others he had seen when he was a mess boy. There were the Headquarters and office area, the officers' quarters, the enlisted men's barracks and, of course, the ever present parade field. The wagon pulled up close to the stable area and stopped. Several noncommissioned officers, all black, and a white captain approached the new green troops.

"Sergeant Daniels, get these people in some kind of formation," Luke heard the captain order.

Master Sergeant Daniels stepped forward. Luke had seen some big men, but Daniels was a giant. Close to six foot six and weighing at least 230 pounds. His brow sort of folded down over his eyes in a row of wrinkles. His jaw was broad and square. Daniels shouted and when he did, Luke expected to see the teams bolt and stampede.

"OK, you bunch of burrhead, sorry sacks of nothing, get your lazy butts off those wagons and line up here. The captain wants to see if any of you are worth making into troopers. Those of you who aren't, he lets me take a stick to you and run you off like a bad dog. Now move!"

The men hurried to line up. As they did, Sergeant Daniels kept up with his intimidating voice, telling them they were stupid and only with his help could any of them expect to learn enough to come in out of the rain. When everyone was finally lined up in several rows that resembled a platoon, Sergeant Daniels turned to face Captain Albert Schultz.

"The platoon is ready for inspection, sir."

Captain Schultz stepped directly to the front of the men. He looked first to the left. His eyes met the eyes of each recruit. When his eyes locked on Luke's, Luke felt a chill run through his body.

"I don't want there to be any misunderstanding," the captain started. As he spoke, he placed his hands behind his back and walked several steps to the left, then retraced his steps to the right. He never, from that first look, looked directly at anyone, yet Luke could tell he saw everyone.

"No misunderstanding at all. I am your captain. If I tell you to jump off a cliff, you had better start looking for the edge. I will give you an order only one time. If you do not respond, I will personally blow your head off. Is that clear?"

There was no response from the men who were used to standing in silence when being addressed by their previous masters. Captain Schultz looked at Sergeant Daniels.

The sergeant stepped forward and shouted, "The Captain asked you bunch of knuckleheads a question. Now he wants an answer, so give it to him. Do you understand what he said?'

A weak, "Yes, sir," came back from several of the men. The sergeant's eyes narrowed. In a voice so low, it was hard to hear, he said, "This ain't your mama's kitchen. It ain't your old master's parlor. This is the cavalry." Then his voice was louder than before. He shouted, "The captain can't hear you! Do you understand? Now let me hear it if you do."

"Yes, sir!" came the reply.

Sergeant Daniels stepped back and Captain Schultz again was facing the men. "You will be trained to be horse soldiers. Not just plain old run-of-the-mill cavalry either. You will be part of the 10th Cavalry. I took this job for two reasons and I'll tell you why. First, there are those who say you black people can't be taught anything except how to plow a field or pick a sack full of cotton. I," he jabbed his chest with the thumb of his right hand, "know that's a bald faced lie. I have seen some brave men during my career and none were better soldiers than a group of blacks I saw fighting in the Civil War. Second, this man's army is my life. No two bit, lazy, good for nothing is going to make me look bad." He tapped his shoulder, "You see this? Well, I want to get a couple more grades before I hang up my spurs and guess who is going to help me do that?" He paused. "I said guess who is going to help me do that."

The men responded in unison, "We are, Captain."

Captain Schultz smiled and turned to Sergeant Daniels. "See, Sergeant," he said. "They can be trained when there is an understanding by all parties."

Chapter 11

Training was considered complete after six weeks. It would, of course, never be completed. There would always be something else to learn. Rumors were spread by the troops early one morning that they would be moving out soon. By lunch time, everyone on the post had received the word. The men were ready to get on with their work. With the exception of three men who just could not work out, the group was intact. The three that were let go had learning problems and just could not relate to the drills required in the cavalry. They had been transferred to the infantry where they would work out much better. Luke talked to one of the men and found that the cavalry would be the worst place in the world for him, since he was scared to death of horses.

The troops would be designated Company E and would be stopping off at an army post in San Antonio. From there, they would go to Fort McKavett. That was all the information they had received.

Luke had made friends with several of the men in his unit, but his closest friend was a young man by the name of Shanks Elliott. Shanks was tall and thin. His former owner had used Shanks for breaking and training horses. Since Luke and Shanks were first-rate horsemen, they both held the rank of corporal and helped train the green recruits to ride.

Like Luke, Shanks had worked with the Army during the war and the commands were not strange to him. On the contrary, they both had a working knowledge of cavalry formations and knew the orders that were necessary to move the column.

Both men were assigned as squad leaders in the same platoon. They knew that if and when they saw any action, they would be in it together. This catalyst bound their friendship.

It was after supper the third day out on their move to Fort McKavett that Luke and Shanks began to talk about what may lie ahead. "You ever killed anyone?" Shanks asked.

"Nope. Never did. Got mixed up in a killing once, but I didn't have anything to do with it. Seems I was chained to a whipping post at the time." Luke looked at Shanks, "How about you? You ever kill anyone?"

Shanks nodded his head. "Yep. I'm afraid so. Killed two old boys that were set on doing me in back in Kentucky." He paused and rolled a cigarette. He struck a match and took a long draw, then exhaled a cloud of smoke. "Sure did," he said. "Made me sick to my stomach after it was over, too."

"You mean to kill them?" Luke asked.

"Had to. They gave me no choice. I was taking a pair of mares to town for my old master. He planned on selling them in town the next day. Well, these two old boys came at me before I got to town. They must have been hiding in a thicket because I never saw them until they were right there. One of them, the one with the gun tells me to get off my horse, while the other one grabs the lead rope out of my hand. Well, I got down like he said when that blame fool shoots a hole right through my side here.'' He pulled up his shirt and showed a jagged scar just below his rib cage. "I got so mad I grabbed him by the leg and dumped him out of his saddle. His horse shied off. He landed on his hands and knees and I kicked him right in the head and sent him flying backwards. The other one had ridden up and jumped on my back. I grabbed him by the head and threw him over my shoulder and began to punch him in the face. Don't know how many times I hit him. Must have been a lot, because when I quit, he was dead. The other one, the one with the gun, I guess I broke his neck or something when I kicked him.

"Well, by now my side burned like fire. I knew I was in trouble because I had killed two white men. If I go home the old man is going to put the leather to my back. If I go to town, the law is going to put a rope around my neck.''

"So what did you do?'' Luke asked.

"I pulled me some grass and held it tight as I could to stop the bleeding. When it got stopped, I finally looked at my wound. That fool's bullet had just cut my skin and didn't go into me. Man, I looked up and thanked the Lord right there and then. I says to him, 'Lord, you saved me once. Can you do it again?' Then I lit out in the direction I had heard the old master say the Yankees were. Sure enough, He saved me the second time, too, because I wound up in a camp and got me a job with the Army. The colonel in charge, he wound up with three good horses, too.'' He chuckled. "The Colonel rode one of them until the end of the war.''

Luke sat in silence while Shanks told his story. He could

tell the taking of a life had weighed heavy on Shanks' mind all these years. Now, he was in the Army headed for the Indian wars and the thought of killing again was becoming a problem. Luke knew that even though he had never taken a life, he would not hesitate to kill his enemy to save his own life.

"Those two thieves back there in Kentucky, they meant to kill you didn't they, Shanks?"

"Sure did. Why else would they shoot me?"

"That's what I mean. If you had not put out their lamps, they sure would have blown out yours and given you a look at the pearly gates, that's for sure. I don't know about you, but for myself, I'd rather be sitting here telling the story than having them sitting in a nice dark bar bragging about blowing some dumb old nigger boy away to kingdom come."

Shanks took a bite off a chunk of dried sausage and offered it to Luke. "You know, I never thought about it like that," he said. "But you're right as spring rain."

Luke refused the sausage as he spoke. "Well, the same thing is true with the Indians. We are supposed to run them out. If it comes down to a choice between them and me, I can guarantee you I plan on being the one who tells the story."

Shanks laughed. "You're right, Luke. I never thought of it that way, but you sure are right. Me, too. I'm going to be the one who tells the next story, too."

Chapter 12

"Luke, we have been training, riding in formation, loading and unloading these guns and who knows what else for almost six months now. We don't even have enough bullets to practice shooting our rifles. Suppose I haven't shot more than six times. Are we ever going to see an Indian and if we do, suppose anyone can hit what he's aimin' at?" Shanks' statement was made as the two men crossed the parade field after mess.

"You ask more fool questions than I ever knew anyone to even think of, let alone ask." The tone of Luke's voice had the ring of humor. "If I knew the answers to half of what you asked, I would be a general instead of a corporal."

Both men laughed and continued on their way to the enlisted men's barracks. As they approached the barracks, they were met by several men coming out in a hurry.

"What's going on here?" Luke asked in a demanding

voice.

"Sergeant Daniels, he wants both your squads down at HQ on the double. I was just coming for you, Corporal Gray." The young private who relayed the message to Luke was a large boy, light in color. He had been one of the slowest to catch on to many of the commands of drill. He was, however, very bright in other areas, such as tracking and reading signs left hours, even days, before on a trail. His name was Albert Stokes, but he went by the nickname of Rattles. Around his hat band were the rattles from four large snakes he had killed on their trip out west. "All the men here, Rattles?" Shanks asked.

"All but the two of you, Corporal."

"Then let's get down to HQ and see what the sergeant wants." Luke turned toward headquarters and shouted, "On the double!"

The men fell into formation and, following Luke, hit a trot. Luke halted the men when they reached headquarters. He and Shanks then went up on the front porch. Before they reached the door, Sergeant Daniels opened it and stepped out to meet them.

"Corporal Gray reporting as ordered, Sergeant."

"Corporal Shanks," Shanks stuttered then added, "I mean Corporal Elliott reporting, Sergeant."

"You men get your platoon ready to ride. You've got to ride escort for a wagon train coming this way. They will be here before dark. You will ride out with them in the morning and stay with them until they reach Fort Concho. At Fort Concho, you'll be relieved and will carry any dispatches the C.O. has back here. The captain has had a report that you could run into some trouble, so keep your eyes open."

"What kind of trouble, Sergeant?" Shanks asked.

"Indians, boy. What other kind of trouble could be out

108

here? Now draw your rations and get your animals ready."

"Yes, Sergeant," both men said.

For the next several hours, the men drew rations and prepared for their forthcoming assignment. Their gear was packed and tack was lined up ready for the next morning. Luke checked everything over twice. When he was satisfied that they had everything they would need, he dismissed his men. In doing so, he reminded them this was the first real assignment given to them and they would perform as soldiers at all times. He knew if any one of the troops failed, it would be himself who had to face the sergeant. That was an ordeal he had no plans to face, not because of someone else's failure to do his job.

Luke lay on his cot looking at the dark ceiling. As the moonlight cast weird shadows across the room, his mind drifted to days gone by, then turned to what could lie ahead.

"Tomorrow I will be in the field for the very first time on a real mission. No more of that training stuff. This is where they know Indians are on the prowl. Time will tell if when the chips are down I'll kill or not." These thoughts filled his mind as he drifted off to a restless sleep.

It seemed as though he had just closed his eyes when the platoon was being awakened.

"Off your butts and on your feet," came the shout from Sergeant Daniels as he walked through the barracks. His demand was followed by his usual remarks. "This ain't no feather pillow job, you bunch of numb-skulls. Let me hear all of those big feet hit the floor before you feel my foot on your asses."

The men, some mumbling under their breath, began to stir and get dressed. Sergeant Daniels left knowing full well his men would be ready in short order. Their training had been intense and this platoon had performed better than most green recruits.

The men fell out into ranks and were ready to get started on their first mission. The wagon train had arrived the evening before and had set up camp in a clearing just outside the post. There were twenty-three wagons in the train. There were eight freight wagons with supplies. The rest were loaded with families headed West. The freight was to be delivered to Fort Concho. From there, the other wagons would join up with several other wagons that had been waiting for more travelers before venturing West. No wagon boss in his right mind would start with less than ten wagons. Even more would afford additional safety if they were attacked by Indians. However, another reason was money. The bigger the train, the more a wagon boss was paid for leading the Easterners to the promised land.

The sun was up and the day was already starting to warm up when the troops rode out to the nearby meadow where the wagon train sat. There were fourteen troopers, a sergeant and a lieutenant in the column. Lieutenant Robert Dixon rode at the head of the column followed by a young black sergeant named John Steelman. Shanks and Luke were riding next to each other with their squads behind them.

Shanks spoke without turning his head, "Well, we've done it now, haven't we?"

"What?" Luke answered.

"We started our first mission and we drew old Iron Jaw for a commander."

Luke smiled. Lieutenant Dixon had a reputation of being a hard man to serve under. He did not like his assignment nor did he particularly like black troopers. The term Iron Jaw came from the way Dixon never smiled, but kept his jaws tightly clinched, which exaggerated the squareness in his lower jaw. The only reason he had accepted the transfer to a western post was the promise of a promotion. He had been a second lieutenant for eight years and longed for a chance at a command. This could be his avenue to that quest. He had been known to take unnecessary risks not only with his men but himself as well in the hopes of being recognized for valor. He had seen it work before and it could mean higher rank and perhaps a transfer to a white unit under his command.

The troops halted and Lieutenant Dixon waited for the wagon boss to meet them. The two men talked a very short time and the order was given to spread out on both sides of the train. The troops moved into position and the order was given to move out.

The morning wore on and Luke was riding next to the third wagon. He heard a voice call his name from the next wagon back in line.

"Luke," the driver called. "Luke, is that you?"

Luke turned around to see a man with a full beard sitting on the seat flanked by a pretty blond lady.

"Luke, is that you?" the man repeated.

Luke pulled his horse up and shifted back. He looked the driver over, then saw something in the driver's eyes that he recognized.

"Edward?"

The driver reached out his hand. "Well, I'll be damned," he said. "Honey, this is Luke, the man I told you about. Well, I'll be damned," he repeated. "I've been looking at you for the last three hours trying to make up my mind that it was you."

"What in the world are you doing here, Edward?" Luke asked.

"It's a long story. When I reached the plantation, they had sold Red Oaks for taxes. Seems my uncle hadn't paid his taxes for some time prior to his death. Once he was dead, Boddy moved in and wound up with the whole thing. I thought about fighting for it, but could tell it was going to be another lost cause. Man can stand losing just so many times.''

The young woman jabbed Edward in the ribs with her elbow. He jumped and realized he had neglected to introduce the two.

''Luke, this is my wife, Lorine.'' As he spoke a baby started to cry back in the wagon, ''and that's our son, Little Edward,'' he added. ''Lorine probably saved my life after you helped me escape.''

Luke tipped his cap. ''We'll have a chance to talk later. Right now, I best get back to my spot or Lieutenant Dixon will have my hide. Probably be best if we don't talk about any escape.''

Edward nodded with understanding as Luke moved back to his slot in the column. ''We'll talk later,'' he said. Luke heard Edward as he told Lorine, ''That's the same Luke that set me free when I was a prisoner.''

When the wagons were in their circle and guards were posted, Sergeant Steelman advised the men to get all the rest they could. He was a seasoned veteran and understood well how rest could evade them in the days to come.

After Luke had finished his day's duty, he found Edward. The two of them sat and talked for over two hours, each giving the other a brief description of their actions since their parting on that rainy night so long ago.

Edward told Luke how he had heard of land that was available for the man who would live on it and prove it up. Luke thought how he wished he had known about that before he joined the Army. He, too, could be working his own land. He had signed up for five years and he knew before he could even hope to have his own place, his obligation to the Army would first have to be met.

Luke stretched out on his bedroll and watched the stars while his mind toyed with the idea of some day having his own piece of land. "I'll raise the best horses in the whole country." He closed his tired eyes and slipped off to sleep.

He had been asleep no more than an hour when two shots rang out in the night. In a fluid motion, Luke was on his feet, gun in hand. He listened for the direction of the attack or orders from Dixon or Steelman. There was quiet except for the sounds of people like him waiting and getting into position for an attack.

The whole camp was up and every man had his weapon. Some of the women also were ready.

"Who fired those shots?" Lieutenant Dixon shouted.

"Post three, sir. I saw an Indian out there moving in on us. I called for him to halt and he didn't, so I shot."

"Where did you see him?" the lieutenant questioned.

"Out there, sir, big as life he was. I think I got him, too."

"Sergeant," the lieutenant said to Steelman now standing at his side. "Double the guard. Have the men keep a close watch on the mounts. Probably a small party set on picking up a few government horses."

"Yes, sir," came the reply.

The guard was doubled for the rest of the night. Daylight came and no other Indians had been seen. Sergeant Steelman walked out to where the guard had shot at what he supposed to be an Indian. He looked around and called the private by name.

"Washington, get yourself over here."

Private Washington approached with his head bowed. "Yes, Sergeant, you want me?"

"You said last night you thought you hit that Indian, didn't you?"

"Yes, Sergeant, I think I did."

"Look at that," Steelman was pointing at a fresh hole in a large cactus that still had juice oozing out of it.

Washington looked at the hole, but said nothing.

"You done gone and killed a cactus," the sergeant laughed.

Several of the men came over and each took his turn at making fun of Washington.

"Well, one thing's for sure, Sergeant Steelman," he finally said.

"What's that, private?"

"I did mistake that there cactus for an Indian, but I sure did put a hole in it, too."

"Yeah, you did that, but next time make sure what it is you are putting a hole in or the lieutenant may just put one in you."

The rest of the day, Washington was the brunt of all the men's jokes. "Tell you one thing, Corporal Gray," he said while they were watering the horses, "next time I see an Indian, I'm making sure I can count his teeth before I pull the trigger."

Luke chuckled, then added, "If you think you see one, do what's got to be done. Better to look dumb than be dead any day, Private."

Chapter 13

Three days passed and no Indians had been spotted. Several of the men thought they might have caught a fleeting glance, but none mentioned it for fear they, too, would be made fun of as Washington had been. If any of them should see what they mistakenly took for an Indian and it turned out to be something else, Lieutenant Dixon would surely have made an example of the mistaken trooper. No one wanted to have Dixon's wrath fall upon them. Punishment on the trail would be swift and sure, but worse than that would be to have civilian women and children witness such punishment. That would cause more humiliation than the men could tolerate. Knowing this, the men remained silent and kept their thoughts and suspicions to themselves.

On the fourth day their guide, a heavy-set, bearded man named Malcolm who rode out front of the train, raised his hand and signaled a halt. Luke could see him from where he was stationed. He had changed position and was riding next to Edward's wagon so that they could talk.

Lieutenant Dixon and Sergeant Steelman both rode up the trail where Malcolm sat on his horse waiting. He pointed toward a ridge on a nearby hill.

Luke strained to see what it was that had caught the guide's eye. The three men seemed to be discussing something. Sergeant Steelman wheeled his horse around and rode back. He ordered three men out of the column, then called Luke to accompany them. They rode back to the lieutenant and Malcolm. They were watching a lone Indian as he sat on his horse. He, too, was watching the wagon train.

"Probably a whole mess of 'em up there, Lieutenant," Malcolm said, matter-of-factly.

"Maybe," the lieutenant said. He then turned his horse to face his troopers. "You men go with Malcolm and check this out. Do not engage the enemy. If there is a sizeable number, get back here on the double. He may just be curious or want to trade. Under no circumstances are you to engage in a fight."

"Yes, sir," Luke said as he saluted.

Malcolm started off at a trot. The soldiers followed. They approached within several hundred yards. The Indian did not move. He just sat astride his pony and watched. Malcolm halted the detail, then raised his rifle, took aim and squeezed the trigger. The .50 caliber Sharps spoke with a loud crisp explosion. Malcolm's horse jumped to the side. The guide grabbed the saddle horn and remained in the saddle.

"What did you do that for!" Luke shouted.

Luke saw the Indian's body as it seemed to fly backwards off his pony. The horse bolted and ran back over the rim out of sight.

"You crazy or something?" Luke's voice had the sound of surprise and anger in it.

"That's one we ain't got to worry about," Malcolm stated and started his horse up the sloping hill where the Indian had been.

Luke rode up behind Malcolm. "The lieutenant said not to engage the enemy. He's going to have your skin for this."

"Wrong, soldier boy. He told you not to engage the enemy. Out here, nobody tells me what to do or not to do. I was out here fighting these red devils when Lieutenant Fancy Pants back there was still tied to his mama's apron strings."

Luke glanced back over his shoulder. He could see the wagons as they were being formed into their protective circle.

The detail reached the summit of the hill. There lay an Indian boy. Luke guessed him to be in his early teens. There was a large hole in the middle of his chest. He was not dead, but was gasping for air. Malcolm stepped down from his horse and walked over to the boy.

"You're a tough one all right," he growled.

The boy made an effort to get the knife at his side. Malcolm stepped on his arm, then knelt down. Malcolm's back blocked Luke's view and he could not see what was happening. The boy gave out a weak sound and Luke heard the pop. Malcolm stood up with the boy's scalp in his hand, dripping blood.

"That's worth ten dollars in red eye in Angel City when we get there," he said.

The boy moaned and tried to roll over. Malcolm was still holding the boy's knife. He plunged it into the boy's neck and gave it a jerk. The Indian boy trembled, then lay still.

"What's the matter with you," Luke said, recoiling from the shock of such a merciless, cold-blooded murder. He jumped off his horse and grabbed the scalp out of Malcolm's hand.

"You gone plumb crazy, boy?" Malcolm demanded, reaching for the scalp.

117

Luke pulled his sidearm and cocked the hammer back. "On the contrary, I think I just got my sense. Now, you get your ugly face back on your horse and get back to the train before I forget what it is you are supposed to do and blow you to kingdom come."

Malcolm climbed back into his saddle, then demanded, "Give me my scalp."

Luke laid the scalp on the boy's chest, then looked up at Malcolm. His eyes had narrowed to tiny slits. Not a word was spoken, but a message was transmitted. A message whose meaning could not be misunderstood.

The other troopers now had their rifles pointed at Malcolm. He knew not to challenge Luke beyond a given point and that point had been reached.

The detail returned to the train and was met by Lieutenant Dixon and Sergeant Steelman. Luke reported just what had happened and how he was tempted to kill Malcolm on the spot.

"I'll take care of that trash," Dixon said as he walked over to Malcolm.

"You fool," Dixon said. "You may just have signed all of our death warrants by killing that boy."

"Why, Lieutenant? Ain't no Injun a good one until he's a dead one. That one up there, he was all alone. I saw his trail where he rode up. He was all alone."

"You didn't see any thing of the kind. My corporal said you shot him when you were two hundred yards away. Makes no difference now. I have known the Indians have been watching us for two days and never made a move to start anything. Now, that can all change. And why? Because a fool wanted to show off. Well, let me tell you, Mr. Malcolm, if an attack comes, you are going to be in the front line. If one person gets killed, you can bet it's going to be you."

"I can take care of myself, mister. I don't need no fancy

John in his blue uniform taking care of me. I hope you and that bunch of nigg . . ."

Malcolm never finished his statement. Lieutenant Dixon's fist smashed into his face and sent him flying. He lay on the ground holding his jaw and groaned. Dixon walked over and looked down at Malcolm. "Get on your feet," he ordered. "If you live to reach Fort Concho, I'll have you tried and jailed for disobeying a direct order."

Malcolm staggered to his feet, "I ain't got to follow no orders from you," he mumbled.

"You may think you don't, mister, but I've got news for you. When you accepted pay back at McKavett, you fell under my command. Now, get out there and lead the way, Mr. Guide, and you better hope that boy was alone because if he wasn't, you are in for big trouble. What little hair you have might dangle from a lodge pole."

Dixon turned to walk away. He stopped and turned back toward Malcolm who was sitting on the ground.

"Oh, yes," Dixon said, "don't you ever call my men anything except troopers."

Malcolm did not respond, but knew full well he had made two very serious mistakes. The first was killing and scalping the Indian boy and the second was speaking disrespectfully about Dixon's troopers. He may have longed for a command elsewhere, but he still had respect for the men he now led.

Malcolm went about the duties of guide as if nothing had happened. Luke could feel the tension even though there were no visible signs. Malcolm was a man that would not forget nor forgive. Dixon had humiliated him in front of the troops and, worse yet, in front of the civilians in the wagon train.

"No," Luke said to himself, "he's not going to forget at all. When he gets a chance, he'll try to get even with the lieutenant and probably me, too. Well, if he does, I'm just going to blow that skunk to the hereafter."

Three days passed and no signs of Indians had been seen. Luke, as well as the others, was on edge. The consensus of opinion among the troops was that someone had surely found the boy and would be out to get revenge.

The moon rose early and was close to full when the wagon train camped for the night near a small stream. A coyote gave his lonesome call in the distance. He was answered by a call further down the valley.

Lieutenant Dixon checked the guards, then advised Sergeant Steelman to place a double guard on the horses.

"They are out there, Sergeant. I've been doing this too long now not to trust my feelings."

"You think they'll attack tonight, sir?" Steelman asked.

"No, they won't attack tonight. Some of them may try to slip in and steal the horses, but they won't come in fighting. Nope. I expect that within the next day or so we'll meet them on the trail where they'll want the one who killed the boy. When that doesn't work, because I'm not handing over that trash, they'll probably attack."

"You mean Malcolm?"

"Yeah, Malcolm. If that fool didn't get us in trouble, I'll be surprised. If they do show up and want him, I'm not giving him up. I plan on bringing him up on charges when we reach Concho."

The lieutenant returned to his tent and Luke could see him writing at his small field desk.

The night was quiet and by morning, the troops were ready to ride. Each was now ready for anything that might happen. Some, in fact, were hoping something would. The day-in, day-out feeling of expecting action and not knowing if or when it would occur was taking its toll on their nerves. Most wished it would come, so it would be over. The anticipation was causing a great strain and the troops were starting to see Indians behind every bush or large boulder.

It was mid-morning when the lead wagon pulled to a halt as it rounded a bend in the trail. Lieutenant Dixon rode forward at a gallop to see why the wagon stopped. Malcolm had been several hundred yards out front. He was now surrounded by ten or twelve Indians. The lieutenant called for two men to follow him as he walked his mount toward the Indians.

"Shanks", he called. "You speak Spanish, don't you?"

"Yes, sir, I do."

"Get up here with me then and let's hope they speak Spanish, too."

The small group stopped about fifty yards from where Malcolm was being held.

"Ask them what they want," Lieutenant Dixon said.

Shanks asked in Spanish, then one of the braves rode half the distance between the groups. He stopped his horse and raised his lance. Shanks interpreted the Indian's Spanish.

"He said his son was killed and scalped. He knows someone on this train did it and he wants the murderer to avenge his son's death. He also said the boy only wanted to see the black soldiers, the ones he had heard of but did not believe were real. He wanted to see the white men with black faces. He said if we give him the killer of his son, the rest can pass. Refuse and all will die."

"Tell him we are not turning anyone over to him. We will try the guilty one and punish him when we get to Fort Concho."

"He ain't gonna like it, sir."

Lieutenant Dixon glanced at Shanks out of the corner of his eye. "Just tell him, Corporal."

Shanks repeated what Dixon had said.

Anger was building up in the Indian. He shouted, "My son is dead! And why? He only wanted to see the white man in the black skin. The ones with white eyes. Now he is no

121

more. The one who killed him will be no more or none of you will be no more. My people will kill you all."

"They got old Malcolm, Lieutenant," Shanks said. "Might as well give him to 'em. Save us a lot of grief."

"Don't think I wouldn't like to," Dixon said under his breath. Then he shouted without turning around. "Sergeant Steelman, can you hear me?"

"Yes, sir," came the reply.

"I want to distract them. When I count to three, fire a volley over their heads." He then shouted, "Malcolm, when the men shoot, you sock the spurs to that nag of yours and get your worthless butt back here."

The Indian out front became confused and his horse began to stamp his front hoof.

"One, two, three!" Dixon shouted.

Several rifles spoke their language of death. The Indians were thrown into a state of panic and relaxed their attention on Malcolm. Malcolm did as he was told and his horse leaped away from his captors. As he raced toward the lieutenant, he noticed the lone Indian, the father of the dead boy, was between him and the soldiers. Malcolm tried to pull his horse to the side, but the brave followed his move and threw his lance. It passed half way through Malcolm's body. He slumped in the saddle, then fell to the ground.

The Indians were now scattered and the one Shanks had been talking to vanished into the brush after seeing his lance hit its mark.

"Should have given him to 'em, Lieutenant." Shanks said.

"Mind your mouth, Corporal, or I'll give you to them. Let's get back. I don't think we've seen the last of them yet."

A shallow grave was dug and Malcolm was buried. One of the settlers was kind enough to read the Twenty-Third Psalm and the grave was filled in. Several rocks were laid as a marker, then the wagons moved on.

In mid-afternoon the train came to a river. The current was swift and the crossing was slow. Luke had ridden his horse into the river about mid-way of the wagon train. He was downstream of a wagon, using it to break the current which made it easier in the waist deep water for his horse to cross.

Edward was two wagons back. He called out to Luke, "See if you can catch us a catfish in one of your boots."

Luke turned around and gave a wave and chuckled to himself. "The truth is, old boy," he said to his horse, "if you get off this gravel bar, I am not only going to have both boots filled up with water before we get to the other side, but the rest of my clothes will be filled up too. That's for sure."

The horse balked. Luke urged him on with his spurs.

The river bar they were using for a ford was narrow but solid. To Luke's delight, there was plenty of room for a rider and a wagon to cross side by side. Luke was half way across when a shot rang out. The driver in the wagon next to Luke fell from his seat into the river. His wife who was riding next to him screamed. Luke's horse jumped forward with a crow hop. Several shots followed and arrows flew from the underbrush. The lieutenant shouted for the men to rally and attack. Luke felt a thud as if someone had hit him in the head with a rock. His ears felt like they would explode from the noise within his head. He felt himself falling, then realized he was in the water. Blackness swept over him. His limp body was caught in the fast moving stream and carried along with its movement.

About a hundred and fifty yards downstream, the river made a tight bend and narrowed down. Here the water increased its speed three or four times its normal flow because of the narrowness of the channel. As Luke's body came out of the turn, it was thrown into some low hanging branches.

His left arm was caught in the fork of a bush. The force of the water washed the rest of his body under the overhanging brush and held him there, concealed except from the water. The high bluff across the river was too sheer for anyone to descend.

The battle at the ford was now in full swing and the Indians were determined that everyone, soldiers and wagon train people, were going to pay a price for the boy Malcolm had killed.

Troops were now on both sides of the river in small pockets fighting a determined enemy. The fighting went on for almost half an hour before the last shot was fired. What looked like seventy or eighty Indians rushed the wounded survivors. Those that were dead were scalped and mutilated. Those that were still alive were killed. The wagons were ransacked. Most of the items were thrown to the ground. Some floated away in the river. A woman's petticoat was caught on a branch of the same bush that held Luke's unconscious body. This helped to conceal him even more.

Edward's wagon had just started into the river when the attack started. His team bolted and leaped into the river upstream from the ford, causing the wagon to overturn. Edward was caught by the leg and unable to free himself. He was, however, able to hold his head above the water to keep from drowning. The worst part he had to endure was watching the others die and not being able to help them, nor himself for that matter.

Once the fighting was over and the battle-crazed Indians went about their scalping and destroying what was left of the wagons, Edward tried to hide himself. He thought he had succeeded when a shout from across the river brought several Indians running. They jumped into the river and came toward Edward. One pushed his head down. He tried to fight them off, but they were all over him, forcing him to keep his head under water.

The last thing he remembered was saying to himself, "Well, Lord, I guess this is the way it's meant to be." A strange calm swept over him where moments before panic had raged. His body went limp and darkness engulfed his conscious mind.

In the distance Edward could hear voices. He opened his eyes slowly. He could tell they were swollen. He tried to get his mind clear. He reached to rub his face. It was then he discovered his hands were tied fast and stretched out. His mind began to grasp what had happened and he could sense what had taken place. He was being held captive. Edward raised his head to look around. He saw a boy squatting next to him. The boy stared, then stood and spoke without turning his head. The words were foreign to Edward. The boy had not finished when an old man squatted down next to Edward and spoke to him.

"I don't understand you. Let me up," he demanded.

The old man said something to the boy, then pointed toward the stakes.

"If we set you free, you no attack?" the old man said in broken English. Slowly, the boy untied Edward's hands.

The old man held a butcher knife he had found in one of the wagons. He pointed it at Edward, then in broken English, he spoke again. "You no move too fast, white one."

"Who are you? What am I doing here? Why did you tie me up?"

"You ask many questions for one who should answer not ask."

"Who are you?" Edward repeated.

"I am called Screaming Hawk. That," he pointed at the boy, "is my grandson, Little Elk. We found you here where the Apache left you to die. I got the water from your body."

"We were attacked at the river."

125

The old man smiled as Edward spoke.

"My wife. She was killed," his voice trailed off.

"I saw where the Apaches killed the white men and the Black Long Knives, the ones we call the Buffalo Men. They are all dead. For some reason, they spared your life and left you here to die."

Edward tried to sit up, but found he could not gain his balance. He laid back and felt his face. It was swollen. His lips were cracked.

"How long have I been here?"

"One, maybe two, suns," the old man replied. He put a wet rag to Edward's lips, then handed him a gourd with a little water in it. He then turned his attention to Edward's leg.

Screaming Hawk placed his hand on Edward's leg. The pain raced through every fiber of his body. He groaned, but wanted to shout.

"The bone is broken," the old man said. "I will fix it." With that remark, he instructed the boy to get a green hide he had on his saddle. He took four small straight limbs and tied them to Edward's leg with strips of leather. "I must put the bone back together." He handed a small stick to Edward. "Bite on this. The pain will be great. You could bite your tongue off. This will help."

The boy sat at Edward's head and placed it in his lap. Then reaching under Edward, he held him around the arms next to his body. When he was ready, he shouted and the old man gave the leg a jerk.

Edward bit into the stick. His whole body jerked. He turned pale and each pore produced sweat. Darkness again prevailed and consciousness eluded him once again.

When Edward awoke, the sun was shining in his face. He looked around. He was inside a tepee. The sun was coming in the top opening. A short, fat woman was there. She mumbled something and sat next to him. She raised his head and fed him some broth. As he ate, Screaming Hawk came in. "You are awake again. That is good."

Edward was now leaning next to a saddle. He looked at his leg. The old man had splinted it, then wrapped it with the green hide. The hide had started to dry and held the leg as if it were in a cast. "You will not walk good on that leg until the leaves of the trees are gone. Maybe not until the green ones come back again."

"I've got to get to the fort. Fort Concho. Can you show me the way?"

"You go nowhere. You belong to us now."

"What are you saying? Who are you anyway?"

"We are the people. We are called Comanche."

"Comanche?" As Edward spoke, fear gripped him with both hands. He had heard stories about the Comanche and none of them had been good. The old man read Edward's face and raised his hand. "Do not fear. No harm will come to you here. Once many winters ago, a white man saved my life when a horse fell on me and my leg was caught under him. That white one freed me and cared for my leg. I stayed with him for one of your years. That is how I come to speak with your tongue. I stayed with him a long time until I could return to my people. So it is with you. When you can ride, I will lead you back to a trail that will take you to your people. Until then, you belong to me and no harm will come to you."

Edward lay back down and looked at the sky through the hole at the top of the tepee. His mind tried to put everything into perspective, but it was no use. Confusion seemed to reign.

Chapter 14

Luke heard the water then felt the pain in his head. As he opened his eyes, he found things were out of focus. He blinked. Slowly things came into perspective. He tried to free his caught arm, but found he was hung up not only in the limbs, but by a thorny vine that had wrapped around his arm several times. Slowly, he freed himself. His head throbbed. Once his arm was free, he tried to pull himself through the brush to the bank.

"That's like a wall," he grunted. "Have to go around." He slipped back toward the rushing current. His feet were swept downstream. He lost his grip and fought the current. Clear of the brush, he managed to crawl ashore where he lay for several minutes trying to collect his thoughts and regain some of his strength.

Slowly, he stood. His strong legs wobbled, but held. He then started to walk back upstream. The thought of Indians still being close did not enter his mind. As he came to a bend in the river, he had to climb a bank. From the top of the bank, he could see the ford. The devastation was everywhere. Overturned wagons and bodies were lying on both sides of the river in ugly, unreal heaps. Some were half in, half out of the river.

"Oh, my God," he said and sank to his knees.

It was then that the thought of danger materialized in his mind. Reflexes sent his hand to his Colt still in its holster on his side. He removed the handgun and cocked it. Slowly, he moved down to the ford. Several bodies lay next to the river bank. They were swollen and had turned color from exposure to the sun. A little girl lay half in the water, half on the bank. Luke pulled her clear of the river and then waded out to a mule still in harness and hitched to an overturned wagon. An arrow in the animal's shoulder was meant to kill him, but the point had struck the collar and was prevented from penetrating too deeply. Luke worked the arrow out and tossed it aside.

"We got to get us some help, old mule. I know it is going to hurt for you to carry me, but you can't be hurting any more than me right now. Besides you and I are all that's left alive." It took some real effort to get the mule free of the wagon.

Luke removed the harness and cut the long reins to a length suitable for a rider. Luke walked, leading the mule until the animal's legs were steady. With great effort, he mounted the mule's back.

"Don't give out on me, old boy. I need you in the worst way." As he spoke, he patted the mule's neck.

Luke had ridden most of the day. He was so tired he thought he would fall off the mule. To keep this from happening, he tied the mule to a small bush and took a potato from his pocket. The potato was the only food he had found at the ford. He ate it raw. Luke checked the mule's wound. He could tell infection was setting in. He made a potion of mud and grass and packed the wound.

"We'll just rest for a spell, old mule," he said and stretched out in the shade and went to sleep.

Luke awoke to find the sun was nearing the edge of the hill and he knew he had to move on down the trail. He struggled back on the mule and rode until almost dark. He pulled the mule up and listened. He thought he could hear something a long way off. His eyes searched the horizon. He saw what looked like a dust cloud.

"It's those red devils again," he said. "We had better get ourselves hidden, mule. If they find us, they'll finish what they didn't do last time."

Luke saw a thicket and rode the mule into it. He dismounted and watched. As the dust came closer, he could tell it was not Indians, but a column of cavalry. Luke mounted the mule and, with renewed strength, he rode for the column.

He met the troops just before dark and told the officer in charge as much of the story of what had happened at the ford as he could remember. Captain Langford had been out west for over three years and knew what to expect as Luke's story unfolded. The parts Luke could not remember, Langford knew from his experience.

"No need going on tonight, Sergeant," he told his second in command. "We'll rest the men and horses here tonight and do what has to be done tomorrow morning. Now, Corporal, we had better get something on that head of yours. Looks like you missed seeing the great beyond by about half an inch."

Luke nodded. "I suppose my head is just too hard for a bullet to get through, sir."

Captain Langford chuckled and shook his head. "No, Corporal, it wasn't your time, plain and simple. When the time comes, no matter where you are or what you are doing, old man death takes you with him." Langford walked away, then turned back to face Luke. "I would send you on back, but we may need every man if we run into those murdering devils again. Besides, I can always use another man who is hard to kill."

"I would rather stay with the column myself, sir, if I could. I had lots of friends back there at that ford. Besides, sir, all I have now is a knot and a cut on my head. I stopped seeing double this morning. I'll be good as new come daylight. All I need is a bite to eat and a little rest."

The captain moved his men out before daylight and rode steady until they reached the river crossing.

Luke joined in and helped pull the wagons still in the river to dry land. Two wagons had been turned over on their sides. Once they were upright, the men rested. Luke sat next to a young private who rolled himself a cigarette. He handed the tobacco sack to Luke.

Luke motioned with his hand that he did not want any tobacco. "You all come looking for my detail or were you just on patrol?" Luke asked.

"Who, us? Shucks, Corporal, I don't think anybody knew you folks were anywhere out here. We were just looking for some Injuns to kill."

"Looking for Indians to kill?" Luke questioned.

"Yep. The captain, he's kind of partial to Indian hunting, so every now and then, we go out and hunt some Injuns. We generally find them, too. He's real good at looking for them." After he finished his statement, two other troopers burst into laughter. "He gets all worked up when we don't find any," one of them remarked.

"What are you talking about, man?" Luke asked. "You mean to say you go hunting Indians the same as you would deer or bear. You just murder 'em if you find them."

132

The private's face turned cold and stern as he looked Luke square in the eyes. "We don't call it murder out here, Corporal. You must be a new trooper, 'cause out here we just kill enemies. There ain't no law against shooting no squaw or brave either. We are going to kill them all. That's what we are supposed to do."

Luke had known hard, cold men and had seen some of man's inhumane acts before, but this was a new twist. Somehow he had managed to remain a bit naive and never thought of murder as a game. Until he had witnessed Malcolm's killing of the Indian boy, he had not seen an Indian in the wild, only the ones around the fort.

Until mid-afternoon, everyone was kept busy burying the dead and recovering what could be used from the wagon train.

Luke looked at each of the bodies and to his surprise, Edward's was nowhere to be found. He walked down the stream past where he had been washed. He came to a log jam which formed a waterfall. The logs held one body that was bloated from the sun and water and a great deal of other items that had floated downstream, but no Edward.

Luke asked himself, "Don't suppose Edward, like me, could have escaped somehow and is wandering around out there in those hills, do you?"

"You say something, Corporal?" Captain Langford asked as he heard Luke talking to himself.

"No, sir. I guess I was just wondering out loud."

"Is that a fact now? And what are you wondering about?"

"A friend of mine was on that train. We found his wife, but there isn't hide nor hair of him anywhere."

"Was he another trooper?"

"No, sir, he was a white man by the name of Edward Lynn. He was the nephew of my old master back in Georgia."

"Bet you would like to find him and even up a few old

133

scores."

"Oh, no sir. Ain't nothing like that. Edward and me, we have always been friends."

"I don't understand you people. Never have, never will. We don't have time to go looking for some civilian who's probably dead anyway. Get that body out of there and let's wrap this thing up." The captain pulled his horse around as he spoke and rode back to the crossing.

The body Luke found in the log jam was buried and the troops were ordered to mount up. The column rode for the rest of the day and camped next to another stream.

Scouts were sent out in three directions and guards were posted. Some time around one o'clock in the morning, Luke was on guard when two of the scouts returned. They went straight to the area the captain had set up as a command post. Luke saw the light from a candle and moved closer. He stood in the shadows and listened as the scouts reported. He heard the scouts tell Captain Langford they had found a small village about seven miles to the northwest. "How many are there?" Langford asked.

"Maybe ten or fifteen, sir. We counted four wickiups. May have been more back in the trees. We couldn't get in too close. Probably a hunting party or a small band moving to better ground."

"See any women or kids?"

"Yes, sir, sure did. Saw two myself."

Luke moved away from the small canvas leanto. He saw the captain putting on his gun belt. As he walked back toward the edge of the camp, Captain Langford came out and shouted, "You there. What's your name, come here."

Luke returned to where Langford stood. "Yes, sir."

"Get the men up. We're moving out."

"Right now, sir?"

"Right now, Corporal. Now get a move on."

"Yes, sir," Luke responded and hurried off to wake the camp.

"I suppose we are going on a hunting trip. Maybe it'll be the ones that attacked us at the river ford. Now's my chance to even up a few things." This thought crowded Luke's mind.

In less than half an hour, camp was broken and the troops moved out. Captain Langford had given strict orders. No one was to smoke or speak while on the march. He wanted their attack to be a total surprise.

One of the scouts had remained to watch the Indian encampment and would stop the detail before it approached too closely. Some would attack on foot and the balance would lead in with the usual cavalry charge.

The first half of the trip was ridden at a brisk pace, then the horses were walked. This would prevent any undue noise in the still of the night and would not alert the sleeping village.

The column was met by the lone scout as they topped a ridge. He spoke to Langford who signaled the men to dismount. Those previously assigned to ground battle picketed their horses and followed the scout. Luke was left with the horses as were four other men.

"When the shooting stops, I want you men to bring in these mounts," Luke was instructed by the sergeant.

Luke and his detail waited for over an hour before he heard the crack of the first shot. It was followed by a steady sound of shooting for several minutes. Then there was an isolated shot or two.

"That's our call," Luke said. "Let's get these horses down to the captain."

The sun was just starting to peek over the rim as Luke, followed by his detail, rode into the Indian camp. The Indians' shelters were in flames. Several bodies lay stretched

135

out on the ground.

Three troopers held a woman down while the fourth prepared to rape her. She screamed and struggled, but to no avail. Luke watched and could not believe what he was seeing.

"What's going on here?" Luke said, as he dropped the reins to the horses he had brought with him. He rode up to Langford. "Captain, what is going on here?"

Langford looked straight at Luke. His expression was that of a mad man. "What does it look like? We are ridding the country of these devils. That's our business. We find 'em. We kill 'em. That's what we get paid for, boy. Now if you plan on staying alive out here, you had better get a move on and see if any got away over in that brush."

Luke felt like he would throw up. He turned and tried to look away. "This isn't what I joined the Army for. Fighting is one thing, but this isn't right. It just isn't right."

Luke had dismounted and remained standing next to his horse for several minutes. Finally he mounted and rode back to where the horses were being held. A young private was holding a picket rope and looking at the ground, his foot moving the loose dirt from one side to the other. "You take part in this?" Luke asked.

"No, sir, Corporal. I ain't never done none of that stuff."

"What's your name, boy?" Luke asked.

"Bitters. Private Jack Bitters."

"Well, Jack Bitters, I think the two of us are the only ones here with a lick of sense."

Luke stood by the horses as the men ran from tepee to tepee. They dragged some of the Indian's belongings out and like crazy men destroyed everything in sight.

A small girl who had been hiding under a pile of buffalo robes was discovered when one of the soldiers jerked the robes off of her. She sat there trembling. The soldiers looked at her with surprise. A shot rang out and the child was sent sprawling backwards. Luke's head snapped toward the sound. There sitting on his horse was Captain Langford.

"You hesitate like that, soldier, and the next time you could be the dead one," he shouted. As he spoke, he returned his revolver to its holster.

"Yes, sir. Yes, sir," the soldier replied and slowly backed away. When there was a tepee between the trooper and Langford, Luke saw him break and run to a group who was putting robes on a fire. Luke's eyes searched the village. He counted thirteen dead women, six children and three old men. "I suppose the young men must be off hunting or something. What a sight to come home to." His mind seemed to flash to a time when in his own life, he had returned to a sight much like he saw here. It had been a few days ago and there when death was all around, there were no fires but the destruction was the same. The difference was those attacking may have had just cause. This did not.

"What is the sense of all of this?" he said half out loud.

"You say something, Corporal?" Bitters asked.

"No, nothing. Just remembering and wondering, that's all."

Langford had the bugler blow assembly. Then he shouted, "Get those rag huts on fire. We've got miles to cover before dark."

When the entire village was on fire, Luke noticed several of the dead women had been dragged to a clump of trees. There they were hung by one leg from a low limb. Their heads were only inches off the ground. Each body had been brutally hacked and disfigured. The bodies of the three old men had been hung by the neck from a higher limb.

"God all mighty. No wonder they hate us so much. There ain't no way a man could ever put this sort of thing right. No way. I know if I came home and found this, all I would

137

ever think about would be getting even.''

Luke was able to catch an Indian pony to ride. His mule was no longer able to carry him. The infection in his wound had crippled him. Luke slowly drew his pistol and destroyed the mule. ''Sorry,'' he said as he pulled the trigger.

''Mount up,'' came the command and the troops moved out. They rode hard for almost six hours, stopping only twice to water and rest the horses.

It was at one of these rest stops that Luke asked Bitters, ''That sort of thing that happened back there, does that go on after every battle?''

''You mean killing 'em all and setting everything on fire?''

''Yeah, that too. But I really meant killing the women, then cutting them up and hanging them in a tree like that by one leg and hanging those old men by the neck?''

''Sometimes worse than that. This here is a mean outfit, Corporal. That Captain Langford is one of the meanest men I ever came across. He's got him a hate for these Indians that goes plumb to the bone. Take some advice from this black boy here,'' Bitters patted his chest, ''and don't let him hear you question any of his actions, else you'll be mighty sorry.''

Luke knew the advice he was getting was sincere. He knew also that Bitters had been around long enough to have seen Langford at his worst. For the next three days, the patrol rode a route Luke could tell they knew and had probably ridden before. At two overnight camps, he had noticed the place the horses were picketed showed signs of having been used before.

It was the afternoon of the third day when the fort came into sight. Luke never thought he would be so glad to see a fort as he was when they rode through the gate. The troops went straight to the corral and after the horses were taken care of, they went to a long barracks where most fell on their bunks.

"I suppose I ought to see the captain about my getting back to Fort McKavett."

"Tell you what, Corporal. If I was you, I don't think I'd be bothering the captain. Not now anyways. He's meaner than those Indian bucks will be when they get back to camp," a private said. His statement was followed by the laughter of several men.

"What are you talking about?" Luke asked.

The young soldier sat up on the edge of his bunk. He leaned over and rested his folded arms on his knees. "I'm talking about the captain. We only found one Injun camp on this patrol. We didn't kill one good buck and, man, that upsets him more than a little bit. He's probably half drunk by now and when he's like that, the best thing is to stay clear of him."

Luke stood up and tucked in his shirt tail. His sleeves were still rolled up past his elbows. The muscles rippled in his forearm. With his shirt now in place, he drew his shoulders back which caused his chest to expand. "Well," he said in a calm voice, "a man's got to do what a man's got to do. I've got me a unit to get back to. A unit that doesn't make war on women and children."

"Talk like that will get you in deep trouble, mister," another soldier said as he stood up. Luke jerked his head a little and smiled. Without another word, he walked out of the building and headed for Headquarters. Inside he found Master Sergeant Dave Early, a large black man with very small facial features. "What do you want, boy?" was Luke's greeting.

"I want to know how I'm going to get back to my unit, Sergeant. They'll be calling me a deserter if I don't get back pretty soon."

Luke had just finished when Captain Langford walked through the door. "What are you doing here, Corporal?"

"Asking about getting back to Fort McKavett, sir, before they list me as a deserter."

Langford smiled. "Don't worry about it, Corporal. I've told the whole story here in my report. I have also asked that you be reassigned. I can always use another strong back and we are still a couple short from a raid we were on last month."

Langford looked at Sergeant Early. "The colonel in there?"

"Yes, sir."

Langford started through the colonel's office door. He stopped and looked over his shoulder. "Find yourself an empty bunk, Corporal, and get some rest. We don't waste time here like those people at Fort McKavett. We'll get our gear together and day after tomorrow, we'll be on patrol again. This time I'll give you a chance to show me what you can do. Now, get out of here." He stepped through the door and closed it behind him. Luke looked at Sergeant Early.

"Well?" Early asked.

"Just like that he can get me assigned here?"

"Just like that," was the reply. "Now, get out of here before he comes out again. If you don't care about yourself, don't think I don't care about me. Now, get!"

Luke walked back to the barracks. His idea of army life had taken a turn for the worse.

"I can't work for that butcher," he thought. Then he realized that he had to or pay the price, and the price was too high.

Chapter 15

Luke lay awake most of the night thinking about what had happened at the Indian village and the killing of the little girl. He remembered how proud he was when he put on a uniform for the first time. Now it made him feel dirty. "They were here long before anyone else. This don't make no sense at all."

When the bugle sounded reveille, Luke was already awake. He dressed and without speaking to anyone went outside. Someone struck a match behind him in the half light of morning. Luke had not seen the soldier standing next to the building until he struck the match. "You look like you may be lost or something."

The voice was friendly and Luke felt it was one he should know. The trooper lit his cigarette and took a long draw. It was not until then that he recognized Master Sergeant Early. "I just may be lost, Sergeant," Luke said.

"That's OK, Corporal." Early walked around Luke as if to look him over. "You didn't cotton to the raid you went on, did you?"

"You want the truth?"

"You ain't the run-of-the-mill trooper. I could tell it when you came into my office yesterday. Nope, you ain't run-of-the-mill at all. I'll tell you what you are. You are plumb stupid. That's what you are. Stupid.

"Now you listen to me, mister, and you listen good. That Captain Langford had just as soon blow your head off as he would one of those red devils. He hates our guts, but he's got to use us to get at the Indians. You cross him one time and you're a dead man. Remember, if he sees you as someone standing in his way, he'll sure as rain is wet move you out of the way. He's done it before." He paused and looked at the cigarette he had been holding between his fingers. "Now if you are as smart as I think you are, you'll do just what you are told to do. No less, no more. You understand?"

Luke nodded as he spoke, "I understand, but that don't make it right."

"Right ain't got nothing to do with it, boy. I'm going to tell you something that may just save your life. Right ain't got a damn thing to with nothin'. That man's crazy. Everybody knows it, but he's got a brother who is a big shot back in Washington, D.C., and nobody from the colonel down is gonna cross him up and get away with it. So, just play his little game and you'll be OK."

"What are you talking about? That man was killing women and children like they were dogs gone mad. This is worse than when they took our people from their homes way back when and clamped chains on them."

Early shook his head. "You ain't listening to me, boy." Luke raised his hand to interrupt Early. "Yes, I am,

Sergeant. I hear every word you are saying. I also understand the point you have made and I know I'm helpless to change a thing. It was the same when I was nothin' but a tadpole and the overseer got mean and whipped up on someone. But I want you or somebody to know that I ain't no murderer. I'm a soldier."

"I know," Early responded. "That's why you have to keep your big mouth shut and go along with this game. Now, if one of these days a stray bullet should find the captain's head," he paused, then added, "now, wouldn't that be a shame. Imagine some dumb Indian managing to blow our captain's head off. Wouldn't that be a shame. I'd probably cry myself all the way to the nearest bar and get fallin' down drunk with grief."

Early dropped his cigarette and crushed it out with his boot heel. Then without another word, he turned and walked away.

Luke watched him until he was out of sight. His mind was rethinking what had been said. He thought to himself, "What was that all about? Do you suppose he was telling me to make sure the captain gets shot on the next raid?"

"Fall in!" came the command. Luke stood in ranks while details were assigned. He was to work in the stables with a detail of seven men. As corporal, he would be in charge.

Captain Langford came up to the stable area after lunch. He was accompanied by a sergeant Luke had never seen.

"Corporal Gray," the captain called.

"Yes, sir," Luke answered as he saluted.

"This is Sergeant Brown. You will be assigned to his platoon. Everything has been taken care of, just like I said it would be. You are now officially part of G Troop, second squad. You will be squad leader. I will expect you to perform exceptionally well after the report I received from your previous commander. Especially since, during the Civil War, you saw how real soldiers function."

"You ever do any fighting?" the sergeant asked.

"Some," Luke replied, not wanting to admit he was really not too battlewise.

"I mean the kind we do out here. Fighting these red devils." As he spoke, he cut his eyes over toward Langford. Luke had his eyes fixed on Brown and did not answer.

"Well, Corporal," Langford said.

"I've been in a couple of scrapes, Captain. Nothing like I was in the other day when we were attacked at the river crossing, but I've seen some action. Back under Colonel Durks during the big war. I was nothing but a civilian and not supposed to pick up a gun. There were a couple of times when I had no choice and did what had to be done."

"Good," Langford interrupted. "I hate to break in a green hand. We will be riding out tomorrow at daylight. Sergeant Brown's detail will ride first scout."

Luke's eyes went back to Brown. "Why is he telling me all this?" Luke thought. I do whatever they tell me. I don't need him telling me what his plans are."

"We ride an hour before the main column, so be ready," Brown said.

Luke nodded. "I'll be ready, Sergeant."

After the evening meal, Luke returned to his barracks and stretched out on his bunk. He was lost in thought when he felt someone near. He opened his eyes to see Private Bitters standing at the foot of his bed.

"You want something, Private?"

"Just to talk, Corporal. That's all, just wanting to jaw some."

Luke smiled and sat up. "Sure. What's on your mind?"

"You'll be riding with Brown, I hear. That right?"

"Yep. That's what the captain said today."

"He's a tough one," Bitters said, "but he's a good one

144

to be with. You watch yourself. He ain't got much love for the captain either.''

"That right?" Luke asked. "Why is that?"

"I'll tell you why. The captain had him jailed about a year ago, but I guess he had rather do his soldiering under the captain than sitting out his time in the stockade. Besides that, he's plumb mean when it comes to going after them Indians.''

The two men talked about days gone by and how it was when they were boys. Luke did not talk nearly as much as he listened. Bitters had found a friend. Someone who he felt saw things the same as he did.

After an hour, Luke said, "I've got to get me some shuteye. We are leaving about four in the morning.''

Bitters stood up and reached out his hand. Luke took it and the two men shook. "You watch yourself, Corporal. Lots of men have died out there on patrol. Some by means other than the Indians, too.''

Luke smiled and nodded, then laid back down. It was some time after three o'clock when he was awakened.

The detail ate a quick meal, then drew rations and ammunition. They were then marched to the stable area.

"Let's get saddled up and move out,'' Brown barked. "We've got a lot of ground to cover.''

They rode in formation for over half an hour when Brown halted the detail.

"OK, men,'' he said. "We got us a new scout here.'' He looked at Luke. "I want you to take Pee Wee and old Hooknose over there with you, Corporal. They'll help keep your hair on your head.'' He motioned to the right. "You people, check it out to the foothills over yonder, then cut northwest to the salt flats. We'll meet up with the captain tonight at Blind Man's Pass.''

"Excuse me, Sergeant, but I don't know where any of those places are,'' Luke said.

'These two do,'' was the reply.

"And suppose something happens out there and I wind up by myself?"

Brown looked down, then raised his head slowly. He spoke in a low, calm voice with no feeling. "I suppose if that should be the case, you will probably get skinned out by some Apache. Now, get to riding, mister.'' Luke pulled his horse out and followed Pee Wee, who had already headed for the foothills.

"By the way," Brown shouted, "if I was you, Corporal, I'd make sure nothing happens to either one of those blockheads." He finished with a laugh, then added, "See you later or maybe some day I'll see part of you hanging from a lodge pole. Best keep them two in sight."

Luke turned in the saddle and rested his left hand on his horse's rump. He watched Brown as he rode off with his part of the detail. He shook his head and rolled his eyes back in his head. Then to himself, he said, "Good idea, Sergeant. Might even surprise you to know that thought already occurred to me." He sat back square in the saddle and gave his mount a slight kick, putting him into a trot.

It was late afternoon when Pee Wee cut an Indian trail. He dismounted and examined the tracks he had spotted. Luke rode over to Pee Wee, who was kneeling down.

"How long ago?"

Pee Wee looked up and spoke in his southern drawl, "Last night." He looked down again and moved a stone with his finger, then added, "Maybe early this morning. Hard to tell for sure. Ground's so blamed dry and we didn't have any dew this morning.''

Pee Wee stood up and looked around. "Truth is, Corporal. They may be watchin' us right now. Those people are like bats in the night. One minute, they are in sight. The next, they are gone." He mounted his horse. "No use standin'

146

around here. One thing is for sure. If they don't want to be seen, we sure ain't gonna get even a glimpse of them."

The three men worked their way along the foothills. From time to time, tracks would be spotted, but no fresh signs. None were any fresher than the first that had been found.

It was almost dark when Hooknose told Luke about a cliff where he had camped before. "There," he said, "we can rest our horses and catch a little shuteye with little fear of being caught by surprise."

Hooknose led the way and weaved through small hills and around gullies to the cave. The shallow cave was just as Hooknose had said. After taking care of the horses, the men sat down and ate their cold meal.

"Wonder what it was like here a hundred years ago?" Luke's question was half to himself.

Pee Wee looked at Hooknose, then back at Luke. "What do you mean by that, Corporal?"

"I mean," Luke said, searching for just the right words, "a hundred years ago there probably weren't too many white people that even knew about this place out here. Sure wasn't any of us out here."

Hooknose chuckled, "That's for certain sure. Ain't no cotton fields for a long way from here. I don't know what was out here then, but I do know most of our kind was somewhere in a cotton field or pullin' corn."

"That's for sure," Pee Wee agreed. "I done picked me a field or two by myself."

"You are a strange one, Corporal Gray. I don't think I ever heard a corporal talk like you before." Pee Wee's statement was more in the form of a question than a general statement.

Luke glanced out at the black sky, whose stars seemed to be close enough to touch. "Nope, Pee Wee, you probably haven't." He leaned back against the side of the cave and

147

stretched out his legs. "The thought ever occur to you two that not too long ago these Indians roamed the whole west and probably the east, too, for that matter. This is their homeland. They've been here for God knows how long. Then we come along and tell them to get out because it's ours. I've got me a problem understanding that. What makes it ours anyway? What right do we have to just say it's ours and that makes it right?"

Hooknose sat up and crossed his legs. "I'll tell you what, Corporal. You keep talkin' like that, you got more than a problem. If the captain even thought you was thinking those kind of ideas, he'd peel your back or bust your head open with his pistol. No, sir, best you keep that kind of talk to yourself, else you're going to be in water too hot to wash in."

"He's right, Corporal," Pee Wee agreed. "We ain't tellin' nobody nothin', but you talk like that and you are really in deep trouble." Pee Wee sat back, using the wall for a rest, his rifle across his outstretched legs. "The captain, he ain't a bad man, Corporal. You have to understand him and what makes him so mean with hate for these Indians."

"Is that a fact? Well, I saw him the other day and I would say he's mean to the bone. What's to understand? He just likes to kill people. Indians especially. It's as simple as that."

"You know him like he is," Pee Wee said. "I knew him like he was."

Hooknose waved a hand, then spoke, "Tell him what happened. Then maybe he'll understand."

"OK. I'll tell him."

"Tell me what?" Luke asked.

"I've known him for a long time. Seems about seven or eight years ago, the captain sent for his wife and two daughters to come out from the East to a post he was at up north of San Antonio. This was, of course, before the big war. Well, somewhere between the Colorado River and Fort

148

Mason, his wife and children were taken prisoners by the Indians. He searched for several years, hoping he would find them. Then one day, his column found a camp. They stormed it and after the killing was over, one of the troopers called him over to a wounded girl. She was maybe fifteen or sixteen years old. She had blue eyes and a papoose lying beside her. She was dying from a bullet wound in her side. She looked up and seemed to recognize the captain. Her last word was 'Papa.' Never knew what happened to his wife and other daughter, but his own troops had killed that one. From that day on, he changed.

"Then the war came along and the government pulled all of the troops out of the West. The captain didn't want to go, but being an Army man he obeyed and was sent into the South. Guess he fought nearly everywhere during the war. Suppose also not a day went by he wasn't thinking about his wife and that other daughter. After the war, he made a beeline back out here. He doesn't cotton to us black folk too much, but that's the only kind of unit that needed any officers. So he came first to Fort Davis. When he got in a fight with another officer, the colonel out there moved him to Fort Concho. Since then, all he wants to do is hunt Indians. He knows if his wife and daughter are still alive, they would be Indians through and through. So he really isn't looking for them any more. He's just trying to get even for all the hurt they caused him. Now, all he wants to do is make them hurt as bad as he has. And believe me, he's doing a pretty good job of it."

"He can't blame the Indians for killing his daughter," Luke said.

"Maybe you couldn't, but he does. They took them to start with and because of that, he's never going to forget. Like he said once, he's not going to quit until there aren't any more to hunt."

Luke settled back. "I see what you mean about thinking out loud. Some things are better left in a man's head."

"That's the way I see it, Corporal," Pee Wee said as he stretched out and closed his eyes. "Some things we can change, some we can't. A smart man knows the difference."

Chapter 16

"Let's go," Luke whispered as he nudged Pee Wee with his foot. After a cold breakfast, they saddled their horses and started back down to the valley. Day was breaking and the world was waking up to another beautiful day.

"About last night," Hooknose said, "best we let all that was said stay back up there in that cave."

Luke nodded, then said, "Don't even remember last night."

It was the middle of the third day on patrol when they met up with Brown at the rendezvous point. They had not found any new trails in the area they had scouted. After the report was made, they headed for the place where the main column was supposed to be.

Just as planned, they met up with the column in early afternoon. Brown reported to Captain Langford, then returned to his detail.

"The captain ain't too happy and wants us out looking for some game. He got a report there may be a camp about thirty miles to the west. Seems like he got a report back this morning that some scout saw smoke up that way. He wants us to check it out."

Within the next hour, Brown and Luke's detail, which included Pee Wee and Hooknose, rode toward the west. They topped a small hill. In the distance, they saw a small column of smoke rising straight up.

"Well, well, well," Brown said. "Let's get closer and check out that smoke. If we found us a bunch of those red devils, we got to get word back to the captain." The valley between the scouts and the column of smoke was perhaps half a mile wide. The trees grew short and thin. There was some brush, but that too was scattered and thin. To cross would mean sure detection if a lookout were posted and there surely would be one, perhaps several.

"Hooknose, you get yourself back and tell the captain what we've seen and tell him about the lay of the land. Draw him a map of where we are. The three of us are going to split up and see if we can find a better way to get close to that smoke. When it gets dark, we'll come back here and go meet the captain." Brown's voice showed strain. He knew he had to find the best angle for an attack. "Hooknose," he said, "you tell the captain I'll send word as soon as I know for sure what is down there, but that I knew he would want to move closer just in case."

Hooknose nodded and rode in the direction the column would probably be by now. Luke worked his way around a small rise and found a gully. He tied his horse to a clump of small bushes. He then crept down a shallow draw, keeping low and moving with great caution. Slowly he followed the draw. Down on his hands and knees, he worked his way to a brushy area. Luke eased himself up over the edge staying close to the ground. He crawled under the brush. There before him was a village. He counted seventeen tepees. Several small boys were playing at the edge of the circle of tepees. Luke lay still, watching and trying to determine how many warriors were in camp.

At the far end of the valley, a herd of horses was grazing quietly. They were being watched by four young men and several small boys who were shooting arrows at a cactus.

Luke smiled and thought for a minute how nice it would be if he could just stand up and walk down into that village. How he wished he could join these people who seemed so free. Leave the Army, Langford, Brown and all he had been exposed to for the last twenty-odd years and become as free as the wind like the people he was watching. As these thoughts raced through his mind, a man limped out of a tepee at the far side of the village. He went to a fire and cut a chunk of meat from a cooking roast. One of his legs was wrapped in hides and caused him great trouble when he walked. He was leaning on a staff and rested on his return to the tepee.

"There's something familiar about that guy," Luke thought. "Wish he'd pull that skin off his back. That fur collar is hiding his head."

The man went back inside his tepee. Luke watched for a while and decided the man was not going to come back out. He started to work his way back into the ditch. All the way back to his horse, he could not get the Indian with the limp out of his mind. He tried to remember every Indian he ever saw back at the fort. He could not put his finger on it, but he knew there was something different about the way he moved.

Brown was waiting when Luke rode back to their meeting place. "Well," Brown asked, "you find a way in?"

"Yeah, but it'll have to be on foot."

"Well, Pee Wee found a way in from the south. I sent

him back to tell the captain and lead him back. I'm going back and watch for them. You get yourself back up there and watch. You go over to that saddle mountain and come in just above the stream. You'll find several large boulders. From the top you can see the village. The captain will be here some time tonight and you can expect an attack just about dawn.''

Luke knew his duty and even though he did not agree with the idea, he would do what was expected. ''Where are you going to be?'' he asked.

''Back up the trail. I'll lead the captain in when he gets here. You be ready. If you see anything that could cause trouble, like a bunch of Indians riding in or something, you get back down and warn me, you hear?''

''I hear,'' Luke said as he started toward the hill with the saddle formation.

With no problem, he found the boulders and positioned himself. He watched. As the day wore on, the shadows grew long and the sun set. Darkness closed in. The moon rose about midnight. With the exception of a few fires burning and the barking of a dog, the village was very quiet.

Luke had watched as several women hung meat on a rack for drying. Luke wondered about the Indian with the limp and tried to figure out what it was about him that reminded him of someone, but it was a wasted effort. The lame Indian never came out, but Luke kept hoping he would so that the mystery would be over.

An hour before daybreak, Luke heard movement coming up behind him in the darkness. He moved to a better vantage point. As he suspected, it was the column led by Brown and followed closely by Captain Langford. Luke met them and advised what he had seen and that the village was still sound asleep. ''No one has come in or gone out,'' Luke reported.

Langford was pleased. He spoke in a hushed voice to his

154

squad leaders and advised them to relay his orders. They would attack at the first rays of the sun and there were to be no survivors.

The men waited and watched. Then the sun broke the horizon and the charge was on, headed by Langford. He screamed and with pistols blazing, he rode straight for the center of the camp.

Luke saw an old man run out of his tepee, both hands raised above his head. A shot was heard and the old man fell back into the side of the tepee. The troops rode straight into the camp shooting everything that moved.

Luke managed to hang back. He felt he had done his job. This butchering was not his idea of war. He saw the Indian with the bandaged leg as he came out of a tepee. He was waving a white rag of some kind and shouting. Luke could not understand or even hear him because of the screams and the shooting.

Recognition finally came to Luke. He shouted at the top of his voice, "Edward!" and raced toward him. Half way to where Edward stood waving his flag of truce, Luke saw a puff of dust spray from Edward's chest. He flew backward. Luke reached him and was out of the saddle before his horse had stopped. He cradled Edward in his arms. Edward opened his eyes and smiled. He spoke in a voice so low that Luke had to put his ear next to his mouth. "These people," he said, "only want to be left alone." He coughed, then added, "Would you look at the fix I've gotten myself in. They saved me only to be killed by my own people."

With this, Edward closed his eyes and his body became limp. Luke, sitting there in the dirt, rocked Edward and shouted, "You people killed my friend!" Luke then laid Edward's head down very easily and rose to his feet. Langford had seen Luke and rode to where he now stood.

"What do you think you are doing, soldier?" he shouted.

"This here is a white man your killers just shot. He was my friend."

"Is that a fact," Langford responded.

"That is a fact you can bet your life on, you crazy killer." As Luke spoke he slipped his sidearm from its holster. He fired from the hip. The bullet struck Langford under the arm and exited out the side of his neck. A surprised look came across his face, then he fell over. Luke grabbed Langford's horse by the reins and swung into the saddle. He drew the saddle revolver Langford had hanging for ready use. With a gun in each hand, he rode through camp toward the corralled horses. Each time he fired, a trooper fell from the saddle.

Brown saw what was going on and charged Luke. His charge was a foolish move. Bitters saw him coming and fired. Brown rolled off the back of his running horse. Luke saw Jack Bitters when he shot and knew he had not aimed at him. He glanced back to see Brown as he hit the ground. Jack then joined Luke and the two of them rode straight for the brush. Bullets whizzed past them as they made their escape. But luck rode with them for not a bullet found its mark on man or horse.

The two men rode for over an hour before they stopped to rest their horses.

"Well, Corporal, we did it now. What are we gonna do? If they catch us, you know they'll hang us for sure. You shot an officer. And me, I did it to a sergeant back there. They'll hang us for sure."

"Maybe, but they've got to catch us, don't they?"

"If they don't get us, the Indians will. We don't have a chance. That has to be the dumbest thing I ever did."

Little was said between the two men for some time. Each was now evaluating the action they had taken. Close to an hour had passed when Luke walked over to his horse. He rubbed the forelegs, then patted the withers.

"I'm going back," he said without turning around.

Jack jumped to his feet and shouted, "You crazy? You go back, they'll hang you right there. You won't even get a trial."

Luke swung up into the saddle. "Not back to the Army," he said. "Back to take care of Edward. I can't leave him hanging in a tree." Luke gave his mount a kick and started back toward the village. Jack leaped into his saddle and followed. They approached the village with great caution and were surprised to find the soldiers had left, taking their dead and wounded with them. Luke noticed that they must have hurried, as none of the Indians' bodies had been mutilated. Edward's body still lay where he had left it.

Luke carried Edward to the edge of the hillside and scratched out a small trench using a stick. He placed Edward in the shallow grave and spread a hide over his face. With his hands, he pushed dirt over the body. He placed rocks over the grave in the hope that no animal would dig it up. When he was finished, he stood up.

Looking down, in a low voice he said, "Well, Edward, my old friend, I placed you in a small wrinkle I made in the flesh of Mother Earth. Maybe, old friend, you'll find comfort there. Lord knows you haven't known too much these last few years." Luke untied the yellow scarf from his neck and wiped his face. He looked back toward Jack who was perched on a rock.

"Get yourself down here!" Luke shouted.

"I don't want to be too close to those dead Indians. What if the braves come back? What then? You're gonna get yourself killed and me along with you. Let's get out of here now."

Jack stood up and pointed toward the north. "There's a town about eighty miles that way. Maybe we can get there together. Then you can go your way and I'll go mine.''

Luke started to walk toward Jack when he saw an old man roll over and try to get up. He had been shot when the raid first started. Without thinking, Luke ran to the old man who was on his hands and knees.

''Hold on, old fellow.'' The words had barely left Luke's mouth when the old man swung around, knife in hand and slashed out at Luke. Fate was with Luke and the cutting edge missed his mid-section by half an inch and ripped a hole in his loose-hanging shirt.

''Here now,'' Luke said as he grabbed the old man's hand, ''all I want to do is help you.''

''You kill Indian. I kill you,'' the old man grunted in surprisingly clear English. Luke saw the wound now and it was bad. The bullet had entered high on the left side just under the collar bone.

''Old man, you need help and I'm gonna give it to you if you want it or not. Now, lie still.'' Luke's voice though firm had a friendly sound to it. He looked back at where Jack still waited.

''Bitters,'' he shouted, ''get over here right now or so help me, I'm going to beat you half to death with a stick.''

Jack approached, but he was slow in coming to Luke who was tending to the old man. ''What are you doing to that Indian?'' he asked.

''What does it look like? I'm trying to save his life. Now, I want you to see if any of the others are still alive. With the captain dead, they didn't stick around long enough to do their butchering. Get to looking or so help me . . .'' Luke did not finish his statement. It was not necessary for Jack was already looking inside a tepee that was partially pulled down. He then moved to a body lying face down. Luke had the old man sitting up and was giving him a drink when Jack approached, carrying a baby.

"Here's one that ain't got a scratch on him. Found him in that tepee over there." He motioned with his head. "There's a squaw back there hurt real bad. She ain't dead, but she's mighty close to it."

"Where?" Luke asked as he took the baby and laid it next to the old man. Looking at the old man, he said, "Watch after him while I go see about that squaw."

"Why you do this?" the old Indian asked.

Luke looked over his shoulder as he followed Jack. "I don't have time to go into that. You just look after that young one."

Luke and Bitters looked at each body. There were four women, the baby, two small boys and the old man that were still alive. They carried them into the one tepee they managed to get set up again. Using a brass pot he had found, Jack managed to boil part of a roast that had been cooking. The broth was fed to each of the wounded.

Luke found some tallow and using some crushed herbs the old man told him about packed the open wounds. It was the best he could do. He knew if any of them were too serious, they needed a lot of help and not the kind a human being could give.

After two days had passed, one of the women was able to help with the others. The old man had run a high fever and at times spoke as if he were already dead and had met spirits of days gone by.

"I don't like this, Luke. We have been here too long. We are going to get ourselves killed, I tell you. Any time now, the others will be coming back from their hunt. Then what are we going to do?"

"Look. We did all we could. We took their dead and tied them in those trees like the old man said. We cared for those we could help. They have to know we aren't their enemy. We tried to help them."

159

"I know for sure they aren't going to look at it that way. They know it was people like us that came in and shot up their folks. They are going to want to get even. If you and me are all they have to get even with, I'd just as soon not be here. We have to get out of here."

Luke thought about what Jack had said and knew he was right. As much as he wanted to stay, he knew they had better get out of the area. If the hunting party did not return, surely the Army would and the last thing he wanted was to be taken prisoner by the Army.

"OK. Get the horses," he agreed. "We'll get out of here."

Jack did not wait for him to change his mind. He ran to where the horses were hobbled. Luke bent down beside the old man and gently shook him. The old man opened his eyes and Luke said, "We are going now."

"Do not go. Stay with us," the old man said just above a whisper.

"I would if I could, friend, but you know as well as I do if I stay, I'm a dead man. When your braves get back, you had better get yourselves lost in these hills, because as sure as the day is long, the Army will be back to finish this job."

The old man reached up and placed his hand on Luke's arm. "You go, but you will be back. I feel this in my heart."

Luke stood up and in a low voice said, "That could be true, my friend, but I just don't see how." As he spoke, Jack called from outside the tepee.

"Come on, Luke, we need to get moving."

Luke turned and without saying another word disappeared through the opening. He swung into the saddle and gave his horse a kick. Before he was clear of the last tepee, he was in a gallop, followed closely by Jack.

When it became too dark to ride any farther, they camped in a clump of trees. Jack had packed several pounds of dried meat he had found hanging in camp. They ate in silence, neither wanting to talk, but both working on a plan to survive after they split up.

Luke was awake early and had built a small fire. The night had a chill in it and he needed to warm himself if only to help him feel better. After daylight, the two men again started riding toward the north.

"What's the name of this town we're going to?" Luke asked.

"Beats me. Don't even know if it's got a name. Rode through it maybe a year ago when we were out on patrol."

"How big is it?" Luke asked.

"Well, to tell the truth, it's not exactly a town. More like a store."

"What are you telling me? We been ridin for two days toward a store and not a town?"

Jack looked off in the distance as if he did not hear Luke's question. After a minute or so, Luke asked again in a demanding voice, "Well? Are we riding toward a store out in the middle of nowhere or not?"

With a silly grin on his face, Jack nodded his head. "Yep. We sure are. Could've been a town if more folks lived there. Fact is, it's not really a store either. More like a place to get a drink of whiskey."

"Well, why did you tell me it was a town if it's only a trading post stuck out in the middle of..."

Luke never finished his statement. A shot rang out and he felt the pain in his side as he fell from his horse. Several shots followed and darkness overcame Luke. He felt he was drifting, then falling into a deep hole. It was as if the earth had opened up and swallowed him.

Chapter 17

Luke heard the rhythm of the drums and the songs of grief before he opened his eyes. He tried to touch his head which felt as if it would split from the pain. It was then he realized he was bound and lying on the ground. He turned slowly and focused his eyes. It was dark, yet the glow from the fires had the area lit to a point Luke could tell he was in the middle of the Indian camp.

An Indian approached where Luke lay. He stood staring at him, then bent down and took his finger and drug it across his face. The Indian looked at his finger, then said something. Of course, Luke did not understand. "That black stays on, friend," Luke said.

The Indian said something else, but this time his voice showed anger as well as his eyes. Luke did not see the motion, but the Indian slipped his knife from its sheath. He grabbed Luke by the hair and drew back to strike when another Indian grabbed his arm. They spoke in loud demanding voices, but the second Indian was successful in out-shouting the first. In a huffed manner, the first Indian stormed away followed by two others.

The second Indian motioned and a woman approached. He then said something to her and she nodded her head. She asked Luke if he spoke Spanish. "Un poco. You speak English?"

"Not too much," she answered.

"What's going on here? Tell these people to untie me."

"They not untie you. They kill you."

"What for? I'm not their enemy."

"You soldier. You kill people in village. You enemy."

"I didn't kill any of your people. I helped them. Ask that old man who was there. The one with a scar on his face. He'll tell them I helped those I could, buried those who were dead. You tell that to this guy," Luke demanded. The woman repeated something to the brave standing nearby, then he spoke.

The woman turned back to Luke. "He says you lie. You kill our people. Now that you are about to die, you fill the air with lies. The old one you speak of is in deep sleep. May not wake up."

"You tell him to ask that old man. He'll tell him I'm telling the truth."

The brave grabbed the woman by her arm and pushed her away. He looked down at Luke and shouted something. Two braves grabbed Luke under his arms and pulled him to his feet.

The pain in his side was like a knife had been plunged deep then twisted to add to the pain. He moaned and felt he would pass out, but somehow he managed to stand. Half walking, half dragged, he was led to a small tree and tied securely to it. His wound began to bleed. He could feel the blood as it ran down his leg.

"Tell you what, big boy," he said to the Indian who seemed to be in charge. "You had better do whatever it is you plan on doing or there just ain't gonna be anybody left to do it to if this bleeding keeps up."

The woman then spoke to the Indian. He, in turn, pointed to Luke's side and told her to take care of it. She ran and picked up a bowl next to a fire. When she returned she reached in and brought out a wad of whitish substance and shoved it deep into the wound. The blood seemed to quit almost at once. There was a sharp pain and the wound felt as if it were on fire. Then a coolness seemed to fill Luke's entire side.

Luke, for the first time, saw Jack. He was tied to a tree not ten yards away. He could see that Jack had been shot also and had been bleeding heavily. Jack raised his head and looked at Luke. "We bought ourselves a passel of trouble, didn't we?" he said. Luke could see where Jack had been bleeding from bullet wounds in his chest.

"How bad are you hurt?" Luke asked.

"Bad enough not to worry about hanging." He tried to laugh but started coughing. When the coughing stopped, blood trickled from the corner of his mouth. "Took me a good one when they jumped us. Thought you were dead for sure, until I saw them tie you up." He took a deep breath. "Knew then you were still alive." He started coughing again and said, "Here I come, Lord." He jerked and went limp against the ropes that were holding him to the tree.

"Sorry, Jack. I should have listened to you and left that camp when you first wanted to go." Luke knew his end was close and if he had ever prayed, now was the time to make some kind of peace with his maker. He looked up and saw the moon. There were a few scattered clouds. He looked back and saw several warriors talking among themselves and looking toward him. All of a sudden, Luke realized what he had seen. It was as if someone had spoken to him from inside his brain.

He looked back at the full moon. The edge looked a tiny bit darker. He remembered hearing about the eclipse. The post commander had explained this occurrence so that none of the men would become panic stricken if they had never seen one before. He had forgotten which night it was supposed to happen. Tonight was the night. The commanding officer knew that many of the black troopers were very superstitious and given to fear of the unknown. There were still many who for lack of understanding and ignorance would panic during a total eclipse and the colonel had said this would be a total eclipse. The moon would be totally blacked out for only a few moments, but it would be completely gone from sight for that short time. Even though it would look strange, this event took place every now and then. It was nothing to worry about.

"Woman," Luke called, "you tell your chief that if he kills me, I will take away the moon and bring great sickness to his people. You will all die. You tell him that now!"

The woman repeated what Luke said. She then faced Luke and spoke. "He says you do not have such power or you would free yourself. He says you speak like a man who eats loco weed."

The pain in Luke's side had grown to such heights he doubted if he could stand it much longer. Being tied to a tree did not help much. He knew he had to hold on if he was to convince these Indians he held the power he had claimed.

"I will show him power!" Luke shouted. "I will darken the moon, but will let it shine once again so he will know that what I say is the truth." Luke looked up at the moon and in a loud voice he said, "My Brother, the moon, hide yourself from these people that would do me harm! Grow black and shine no more if they kill me. If they release me, again show your face so that all who see this will know I speak the truth.''

The woman quickly repeated Luke's words. Everyone in camp looked up at the moon. The drums stopped and quiet swept over the entire camp. Then a gasp was heard, followed by others. The shadow slowly crept across the moon's face. One of the women ran to Luke and cut him free. As she did, the entire moon was hidden from sight. Near panic swept over the camp.

"Tell them not to fear. I will live true to my word." He raised his arms toward the heavens and called, "Hear me, my brother! I am free! Return to light the sky with your face. Show these people that I am their friend and will help them. I am not their enemy, but their brother."

The woman spoke to all now and not just the leader. As she repeated what she could, the moon started to reappear. Again, a quiet hush seemed to ascend and every eye watched until the shadow was clear and a full moon again lighted the heavens. A great howl went up from every soul. They were satisfied that the Great Spirit was pleased that they had spared Luke's life.

Two braves rushed to Luke and grabbed him just as his knees started to give way. They carried him to a tepee and laid him down. Three women stripped his clothes and started to pack his wound with the white substance. An old man sat nearby and chanted while he shook a rattle. This went on all night.

When Luke awoke he looked around to find several men watching him. The woman who had been his translator was there also. She wiped his face with a damp cloth. Luke recognized an old man half sitting, half lying, next to the tepee wall. It was the old man he had helped. Luke smiled. The old man smiled back.

167

"I am glad you did not leave us. I was not told of your presence until after your magic. I was in a sleep. Now I know why I live. Your medicine is strong. My heart is happy you came back and are still alive."

"Me, too," Luke answered. "Where were you last night? You could have told these people how I helped you."

"I was in a deep sleep until the sun came up." The old man used his hands as he spoke. By doing so, the others could understand what was being said.

"We were found by one who returned early to our camp. Word was then sent to the hunting party. Two Feathers found you and your friend before they reached this camp. I was unable to tell him of your help. My body was filled with fire, and I slept. I was unable to tell even the scout. I have lived with the fire in my body and slept until today's sun. I was too weak to tell the story of your help. Your magic has chased the evil from my body." The Indian Luke had decided was the chief said something to the old man.

"Is that Two Feathers?" Luke asked.

The old man nodded. "He said that when your wound has healed, you will be free to go. I told him of your help and he has called you friend. Your medicine is strong and he hopes you will share it with us before you leave."

"Well, you tell him I don't have a place to go. What are the chances of me staying right here with you folks? Who knows? I may even be able to help in some way."

The old man spoke and as he did, his voice seemed to rise to a high pitch. When he finished, he sat back as if to say, I have spoken. This was followed by heads turning from one to another. There was a lot of debate, then Two Feathers raised his hand and spoke. As he talked, his voice was directed at Luke. When he finished, he too sat back and folded his arms.

The old man moved closer to Luke. His voice was low

as he spoke. "Two Feathers has said if you stay with us, what can you do? You are not Indian. You will be like a man on the prairie with no moccasins. We cannot feed a man who cannot hunt, a man who will not kill our enemy, the long knife."

Luke smiled and reached out, taking the old man's forearm. "You tell him I am a warrior. I am a hunter. I am from a far land and when I was but a boy, I like him learned to hunt for food. The blood in my veins runs true to that of his own. My skin may be black, but my blood is red. My heart, true to my word. I will teach him and his braves to fight the same as the long knife. I and only I can save his people. I can show him many things. Since I have lived with the white man I know his ways, his weaknesses. I am the brother to the moon and he has given me much medicine that I will share with your people. These things I will do. Tell him that."

Luke released the old man's arm and watched Two Feathers as the old man spoke to him. The old man's eyes never left Luke as he spoke. Two Feathers responded. His response was short and Luke could tell it was to the point.

The old man nodded and he said to Luke, "He welcomes you and your knowledge. Together, we will rid our land of this sickness. The blue coats with long knives." Two Feathers took his knife from its sheath and cut his left palm. He placed it on Luke's open wound. Each of the others in the tepee followed, then sat back. The old man then cut his hand and placed it on Luke's side.

"We are now one. You are a brother to all who are here. I have been told by Two Feathers, you are to be called No Moon. First, because of what you did last night and, second, because your skin is the same as the night with no moon."

Luke smiled and lay back down. He had been resting on his elbow. "You tell him No Moon must rest if we are to regain what has been taken away."

Chapter 18

Luke slept for almost the entire day. He was awakened several times and fed broth. After he ate, he fell asleep again. It was some time the next day when he awoke. He felt like he was lying in a puddle of water. His fever had broken. Each pore was now voiding his body of fluid.

The old man was sitting not far from Luke. He smiled and said, "Now you will recover the same as Screaming Hawk. Your body has thrown off the sickness of fire. I will tell Two Feathers that we can travel now. We must go far away to the flat lands."

Luke, still too weak to sit up, just smiled and nodded his head. It seemed that the camp was ready to move in no time. Luke was placed on a travois. He noticed there were several others. Each had someone on it. The woman who had spoken for Luke was at his side. She would be leading the pony that was to pull him.

"How are you called?" Luke asked.

Almost girlish, she blushed and hung her head as she spoke. "I am called Gray Dove."

"Gray Dove, huh? Well, Gray Dove, you see to it that this pony gives me a good ride and I'll pick you a hand full of posies when we get to wherever we are going."

A puzzled look came across Gray Dove's face. "Posies?" she asked. "What is that? Posies?"

Luke chuckled, then said, "Flowers. It's just a saying I heard somewhere. It means I'll reward you for a job well done. Maybe if I said I'll bring you a buffalo tongue, it would have a better meaning to you."

"You would bring me a tongue?" There was excitement in her voice as she spoke.

"I will, when I am able to hunt. I will bring you the tongue of the first buffalo I kill." Two Feathers rode by and spoke a few words to Gray Dove. He then gave a shout. The entire camp moved out, following their chief.

The next three days were rough and many hills were crossed. Twice small streams had to be forded, but the water was shallow and posed no problem. The fourth day found the tribe on a flat rolling plain. As they rested during the heat of the day, Two Feathers approached Luke and handed him a chunk of dried meat. He squatted down and drew several lines in the dirt. He spoke to the woman in Comanche and he directed his words toward Luke.

"He asks if you know where you are on the great flat land."

"Tell him I have no idea," Luke responded.

"Two Feathers has told me to tell you we go to a secret place known only to the Comanche. We call it the Place of Arrow Wood."

"How far is it?" Luke asked.

"Maybe as many suns as you have fingers plus this many."

She flashed one of her hands, then one finger more.

"Sixteen days?"

She shrugged her shoulders and said, "Not know sixteen. This many." Again she showed sixteen fingers.

Two Feathers rose and said something, then left.

"What did he say?" Luke asked.

"He asked when you would be able to ride a horse."

"What did you tell him? I'm ready to ride now."

"You are not ready." Her statement was matter-of-fact. "You not be ready for four, maybe five, suns. Then you must not ride for long time. Your side is better, but still not well."

"You're a hard woman, Gray Dove. And to tell the truth, I don't plan on getting you upset with me. If I did that, who would talk for me? That brings up something else. How is it you speak such good English?"

She did not answer his question. She turned and looked toward Two Feathers. "That is something else Two Feathers said. I am to teach you to speak for yourself."

Luke raised up on his elbows. "Speak for myself? You mean learn the language? The language of the Comanche?"

"Yes."

He laid back down and stared into space. "I can't do that."

"You speak your language. You speak some Spanish. Why do you say you cannot learn to speak with Comanche words?"

Luke thought about that for a minute. "You are right. I can learn. It ain't going to be easy. I know that from the grunts I hear."

The rest of the trip was slow, but travel was easy and steady. They moved early in the morning, then at mid-day, they rested. In late afternoon they were again on the move, until almost dark. Each day was much as the one before. The pace was slow, but steady. Wherever they found

173

themselves at dark was where camp was made. Luke had no idea of the vastness of the prairie, the endless stretch of nothing except low rolling hills that seemed to have no end.

After a week, Luke was given his old horse and saddle by Two Feathers. His lessons in the Comanche language had started and to his surprise, the words seemed to stick in his mind. He was now picking out words spoken that he recognized. Not many, but a few.

Gray Dove's lessons continued and she spoke to him almost as much in the Comanche language as she did in English.

It was after they had been traveling for almost three weeks when Luke was invited to sit with the men. A pipe was lit and passed from one to another. Each took a puff and then passed it to his neighbor. Luke sat between Two Feathers and Screaming Hawk. The old man's wound, like his, was healing well. When something was said that Screaming Hawk thought Luke should know, he would relate it to him. Luke was amazed at how much he understood by catching a word here and there.

The men spoke of dreams they thought important. Dreams of a land with no white men. Lots of horses and green grass for grazing. After perhaps an hour of these stories, Luke told Two Feathers that he too had a dream. Screaming Hawk translated and Two Feathers motioned for Luke to speak.

He pointed to himself and started. As he talked, he used what sign language he knew and had managed to pick up since being with the tribe. When he could he would interject a Comanche word. From the expressions on several of the men's faces, Luke could tell they were pleased.

"When I was taken captive by the Comanche I was in a place of darkness. I seemed to be falling, then I stopped. Before me was a cave. The opening was dark yet I had to go inside. I walked into the darkness of that cave, yet it was not dark once I was past the opening. I could see. Blocking

174

the trail in this cave were three snakes. Large snakes. Larger than any snake I ever saw. They were very long, as long as a rope tied to a staked horse.''

Luke paused and looked at each face sitting in the circle. The eyes were fixed on him and they listened to his every word. Screaming Hawk responded and repeated Luke's words so that all would understand. Several whispered something to the one sitting next to them.

"What happened then, No Moon?'' Screaming Hawk asked. No Moon. This was the first time his new name had been used. He liked the sound of it. Somehow being called by his new tribal name made Luke feel that he too was a Comanche, or at least nearing acceptance. At last he felt he fit somewhere. Not for a long time had he felt that feeling. If he had, it was so long ago that it was long since forgotten.

"I will tell you. Beyond the snakes stood my father. He has been dead for many years. Yet he was alive and though he did not speak with his lips, he called to me. He said, 'Do not fear, but come and follow me.' I started, but the snakes grew wild and swung back and forth blocking the way. I was filled with fear. Again my father called me by my name and said, 'Come, my son, trust me. Do not fear what blocks your way. No harm will come to you.' Again I started. But this time, I did not feel any fear and walked to the snakes. They drew back and lay very calm as I walked by. I then followed my father through the cave to an opening.

"Here I stood and looked out on a valley green with grass and a stream that ran through it. Many people were there. They stopped doing what they had been doing and looked up at me. I saw many faces from my past. Faces I had forgotten. They were all there in this valley.'' Luke stopped again and looked at Screaming Hawk, who began once again to translate to those present. Luke could see the interest his dream had for the men from the expression on their faces.

When Screaming Hawk finished he looked at Luke, but said nothing.

"Then, my mother appeared. She raised her hand and commanded me to stop. I did as I was told. 'It is not time for you to come to this place,' she said. 'You have much yet to do. You must go back and complete your task, then you may return.' I wanted to ask her what task I was to do, but I awoke to the sounds of the drums and the death chants of the tribe. I have wondered what could be the meaning of this dream. Perhaps some of the wise ones of the tribe can tell me."

Luke sat back and watched as heads were put close together and hands flew with conversation. Two Feathers then pointed toward an old man who was bent with age. His face was covered with wrinkles from the weather and a hard life. His white hair was braided into two long braids and each held an eagle feather. The old man spoke and from time to time pointed toward Luke. When he finished, Two Feathers spoke to Screaming Hawk.

Screaming Hawk cleared his throat, "No Moon, the father of Two Feathers, Soaring Eagle, has spoken and he has said that you have visited the land of the Great Spirit. You have been given a vision that only a few have been given. When you followed your father and passed the snakes, you showed bravery and trust. When you saw and heeded your mother's words, you showed wisdom. When you awoke and heard the drums, you were shown the way. You are to lead us to victory. You were sent to us by the Great Spirit and in ways of war, you will teach us to overcome our enemies. This is what he has said. Soaring Eagle has spoken with many spirits and his word has always been true."

Two Feathers took the pipe again and lit it with a stick from the fire. He stood and took a puff. He blew the smoke in each direction, starting with the south. He sat down and handed the pipe to No Moon.

"You will do as Two Feathers. Blow smoke to each of the four winds, then blow a puff straight up to the Great Spirit."

No Moon did as he was told. When he blew the last puff, the men all shouted and pulled him out of the tepee. They shouted and danced around him. A buffalo robe was placed on his shoulder and Two Feathers handed him a tomahawk.

"You are now more than just a Comanche," Screaming Hawk said. "You are now a war chief. All of these warriors will follow you in war. They shout thanks to the Great Spirit for delivering you to us. They say you will lead us to victory over the white men."

Luke placed both hands on the shoulders of Two Feathers. Speaking to Screaming Hawk, but looking into Two Feathers' eyes, he said, "Tell him I will lead my new people against the enemy, both red and white. We will drive them from the plains. Only the Comanche will be left when we have finished. I am now Comanche. This is my land now, as well as the Comanche. The land of those before us. All others must go. Then and only then, we will hunt in peace and live as we were meant to do. Tell him I accept him as my chief and I will lead only when he tells me to do so."

Two Feathers listened as Screaming Hawk repeated No Moon's words. Then he said, "You are Comanche. When your body has fully healed, you will ride and we will reclaim what is ours."

Chapter 19

For the next several months, Gray Dove and Screaming Hawk spent each day teaching Luke the customs and the language of the Comanche.

"You are not of this tribe. I mean, you were not born to this tribe, were you?" Luke asked Gray Dove one day.

She smiled, then looked into the distance before she spoke. "I am Comanche," she said.

"I know. But you were not always, were you?"

"No. I was not." She hesitated and seemed to be searching her mind for a memory long put to rest somewhere in her deepest thoughts. Luke watched her and remained silent. He had probed her mind and knew she would answer in her own way and in her own time.

Gray Dove sat down and picked up a half-sewn moccasin and began to finger the stitches as if tightening them. Her voice was low and there was a sound of melancholy as she spoke.

"Many winters ago, when I was but a small child, I had two brothers. One was older, one younger. We lived in a small village in the land you call Mexico. The land where from the beginning of time the Comanches went when the snow flies. I remember little of that time now. It was so long ago. Soaring Eagle came to the village and took my brothers and me away. My younger brother died that first winter, but my older brother and I lived. Soaring Eagle took us into his tepee and we became his children.

"Three, what you call, summers ago, my brother was killed in a raid to get horses. He was wounded and the Mexican who took him tied a rope around his neck and then tied him to a tree limb. He was found and cut down but it was too late."

A tear rolled down her cheek. She wiped her nose using the back of her hand.

Luke reached over and took her hand. She could feel the compassion and caring in his grip. For a moment she became confused. Never before had she seen a man show any sign of compassion. She wanted to draw away, but found comfort in his action.

"Your brother is now in a much better place. You know that, don't you?"

"He is not. When they tied that rope around his neck and pulled it tight, they closed off his spirit."

"I don't understand. What do you mean, they closed off his spirit?"

"When an Indian dies like that, his spirit is forever trapped in his body and he cannot escape."

Luke wanted to tell her this was not true, but thought better of trying to change her religious beliefs at this time. With his finger, he gently wiped the tear from her cheek, then said, "What is done is done and we cannot undo it. Maybe some

180

things are meant to be and we must accept them. The things we cannot change, we cannot change. We must live for today and tomorrow. Yesterday is gone forever." He realized that he had spoken in Comanche.

His use of the language had surprised him. He was now able to understand a great deal, although speaking was still very difficult. He could get a thought across, but still needed help when he spoke in detail; however, his statement to Gray Dove was surprisingly very good and entirely in the Comanche language.

As he sat there with Gray Dove, Two Feathers approached. He handed Luke his army rifle, the one he had when he was shot.

"We go for buffalo," Two Feathers said.

Luke looked at his rifle, then at Two Feathers. "Where did you get this?"

"From you. The day you came to us." There was no mention of his capture. "We go now. Scouts have come to camp with news of big buffalo herd two, maybe three, suns from here."

Luke stood and followed Two Feathers. Several braves were already mounted. Soaring Eagle approached Luke. He dipped his fingers into a bowl of white paint and made two lines from the left temple down to Luke's chin. On the right side of Luke's face, he drew two lines from the bridge of his nose almost to his ear.

"These lines on your face will give you strength and help you to be successful on this your first hunt." The old man then stepped to Two Feathers and made the same design except it was placed on the opposite side of the face. He stepped back and said, "You two are now as one on this hunt. Watch after your brother," he ordered Two Feathers. "He is young and has yet much to learn."

Two Feathers nodded and swung onto his pony.

Luke mounted the horse he had been riding when he was shot. The government saddle was on the horse. The horse and saddle had been given back to him on the trail when he was able to ride. He had ridden several times bareback, but had not come close to mastering it as the Comanches had.

"Some day," he said to himself, "I'll fool them all and ride like they do. But for this hunt I had better use good sense and be thankful I'll have something to hang on to."

They rode hard and rested around midnight. Before daylight, they were again moving to the southwest. Just before dark, they stopped and watered the horses.

"We stay here tonight. Tomorrow, we will see the buffalo," Two Feathers said.

A fire was built and the men sat around it talking. The conversation centered around other hunts. One brave told about the time a buffalo had gored a horse out from under him. He told how another brave had saved him from certain death by dashing in and grabbing him as he jumped on behind him.

It was sometime before daylight when the party rode slowly down a draw. They topped a ridge close to mid-day. Luke had never seen a herd of buffalo and never expected to see such a sight. There grazing in the valley were what he estimated to be over a thousand head. Their brown color stretched over the nearest hill. The small valley was packed with the herd of bulls, cows and calves.

The hunting party dismounted and crept to the edge of the crest and watched. Two Feathers pointed to a large bull and said, "He will be the chief bull. We will not kill him. We need him to father the herd."

Luke had already found out one thing. He had seen that the Comanche bred their horse herds and now he saw they treated the buffalo with the same respect. A herd would be as good as the breeding stock. To kill off the best would

182

deplete the herd.

"What do we do now?" Luke asked.

"We wait. I will send several braves to the other side of the herd. When they are ready, they will ride into the herd and drive them to us. When they do, we will ride in and take the buffalo. When the hunt ends, the women should be here and we will have much meat and robes for the winter."

Four braves rode to where Two Feathers had directed them. The rest lay and watched. Very little was said and then only with sign language. Luke saw the dust made by the braves before he saw the riders. They came over a rise waving blankets over their heads and shouting. The herd seemed to bolt together and started to run toward the waiting hunters.

Each hunter, now mounted, laid down on his horse's neck and watched. When the herd was where Two Feathers wanted it, he gave a shout and charged. He was followed by the others. Each brave selected his own target and went after it. Luke saw a big bull and dug his heels into his horse's side. He raced up beside the animal and fired his rifle into the back of his head. The bull's front legs collapsed and he tumbled head over heels. Luke reloaded as he rode. He spotted a young cow and tried to overtake her, but his horse was becoming winded. He stopped, took aim and fired. To his surprise, she turned just as he pulled the trigger and the bullet flew by her large head. Again he reloaded and started after another animal. His horse was now blowing hard from the run he had been put into. Without notice Luke found he was flying through the air. His horse had stepped in a hole and both rider and mount were now lying on the ground. Buffalo were all around him. Luke found his rifle and shot. A cow went down. He reloaded and dropped a calf. He reached into his pouch for another bullet. It was then he realized that the pouch had come open when he fell and his ammunition was scattered on the ground. He looked around and saw a shell. He grabbed it and was loading when he looked up to see a cow with her head down charging him. There was no time to load. He dove to the side as she passed him. Luke scrambled to his feet. The entire herd was now in a stampede. Everything in its wake would be trampled and he was on foot.

Perhaps thirty yards away was a small ditch. He raced for it and dove for safety. The herd thundered by. Several buffalo jumped over him. The ground shook from the pounding hooves. The level of noise rose to a great height, then it was quiet. The only thing Luke could hear sounded like distant thunder.

Slowly he raised his head. He was covered with dirt. He peeked over the rim. The first thing he saw was Two Feathers sitting on his horse looking at him.

"It is hard to hunt buffalo from there."

Luke stood up and brushed off some of the dirt. "It is very hard," he answered.

Two Feathers laughed and rode up to Luke. He extended his arm and Luke swung up behind him.

"I saw you go down, but could not get to you. I also saw you kill your first buffalo. I will remind you that you promised my sister his tongue."

"I have not forgotten, my friend. And speaking of your sister, I have been wanting to ask you something."

"Oh? What is that?"

"How does a man go about getting a wife? No one has told me."

Two Feathers chuckled. He turned and looked over his shoulder. "Now that you have killed a buffalo, you yearn for a wife?"

"No. Nothing like that." Luke thought for a moment, then added, "Well, maybe I do for that matter." After thinking about what he said, he felt it may be misunderstood. He quietly added, "But I would like to know how a man goes about getting a wife."

Two Feathers turned back and looked straight forward. He said, "First, you must be admitted into a clan. You will have to be tested and prove your worth. If you wish Gray Dove, you will need many horses. Soaring Eagle will not give her away cheaply."

"You mean he will sell her for horses?"

"No. We do not sell our women. The horses will show that you can provide for her. It is for Soaring Eagle you give horses, not for Gray Dove. Before you can even think of such a thing, you must first be taken into a clan. Then you must go on a raid and get many horses. Then you can ask to be joined with a woman. I warn you now, my brother, be sure that is what you want. Gray Dove is not like her name. She can sometimes be like a wild cat. It will take many horses before Soaring Eagle will give her up."

They had reached Luke's first kill. He slid off the horse's rump. "Well, how do I get into a clan? I sure do need me a wild cat."

"You worry about the wrong thing, No Moon. Right now, you need to finish what you have started. I will show you, then when the time comes, we will see about a clan." Two Feathers reached for the empty pouch hanging around Luke's waist. "Give that to me," he said.

Luke untied the pouch and handed it to Two Feathers. He opened the buffalo's mouth. He reached deep and cut out the tongue. He placed it in the pouch and handed it back to Luke.

"A debt is paid," he said.

Luke said nothing, but tied the pouch back to his waistband. He would have preferred to do that himself. He understood, however, that Two Feathers' action was meant to protect Luke's interest and keep him in good stead with

Gray Dove.

Two Feathers then opened the underside of the buffalo. He reached in and pulled out the liver. He cut it free and took a bite. He handed it to Luke. Not wanting to shame Two Feathers, he too took a bite. He chewed it and managed to swallow. The thought of eating raw liver did not appeal to Luke, but it appeared to be the custom.

"We now have to clean the bodies of everything we killed. We will save only those parts we can eat. Be sure to cut the neck and take this out." As he spoke he removed the animal's windpipe. "If this is left, the meat will not be good. When the squaws get here, they will finish, but some things must be done now."

Luke nodded that he understood. Two Feathers then jumped to his horse's back and rode toward another downed buffalo. Luke finished field dressing his bull, then walked to the cow that he had killed. He proceeded to field dress her as he had been shown. This time, he reached in and pulled out the liver and took a bite, then laid it aside. When he finished he found his calf and repeated the process. He had just finished when Two Feathers returned leading a horse.

"You can have this horse, but you will have to leave your saddle. It is much too heavy."

"I know," Luke said. "I think that is what helped to cause my horse to become winded early. That is probably why he fell like he did. When I rode with the Army, we fed the horses grain. Now, we have only grass for them to eat. They tire sooner and that extra weight does not help."

A fire had been built on a hilltop and the smoke rose straight up in a column. Two Feathers pointed to it.

"The signal has been given. The women will be here soon to skin and cut the meat. We will smoke some here, then move the rest back to the Place of Arrow Wood. We will eat good when the snow flies. We have had a good hunt.

186

Your presence has caused the Great Spirit to smile on us. This is the best kill we have had for many hunts. Except for your horse, no one was hurt. On our last hunt, we lost three horses and two braves."

The hunt had been good. Over fifty buffalo had fallen to the hunters and there would be meat for every lodge when the dividing was over.

As Two Feathers said, the women and children arrived shortly after the signal had been given. They went straight to work. Gray Dove went to Luke's kill and began to skin the bull. "Here. Let me help you," Luke said.

She looked up and her eyes narrowed. She responded, "This is woman's work. I do not ask to kill the buffalo. You do not ask to skin him."

Luke realized he had almost crossed a line he had not even known was drawn. Quickly, he untied the pouch he had and handed it to her. As he did, his quick mind saved him once again.

"Perhaps you misunderstood me. My Comanche is still very bad and I lack the ability to express myself. I did not want to help you skin the buffalo. I wanted to make your work easier by giving you a gift." He handed the pouch to her. She opened it and saw the tongue. She looked and saw it missing from the bull. A smile crossed her lips.

"It is I who misunderstood," she said. "My work will be easier now." She lowered her eyes, then without looking up she added, "Go to the men. I will tell you when the meat is ready to be moved."

Luke rode his new horse to the place Two Feathers and several other hunters lay in the shade of several big boulders. Each of the hunters had blood on his face, arms and body. They laughed and relived the hunt, each telling his own story.

"I have talked to the braves of my clan," Two Feathers said. "I am to put you to the test when we return. If you

187

pass, you will be a member of the Owl Clan. We will then go on a horse raid. When we return, you can talk to Soaring Eagle about that matter of which you spoke. That is, if you want to catch a wild cat.''

A smile crossed Luke's lips. He nodded and asked, ''What kind of test?''

Two Feathers did not answer him, but looked at another Indian who chuckled and said, ''A test to see if No Moon is worthy of the clan. You will learn things about yourself you have never known. This test will show if you are worthy to be accepted into the Clan of the Owl.''

Luke looked into the eyes of the Indian and asked, ''You went through this test?''

''I did.'' He threw out his chest and raised his head as he answered.

Luke thought, ''If you did it, friend, I don't see any problem in me doing it.'' But he selected his words wisely and said, ''As with you, if the Great Spirit wants me to pass this test, I will.''

He turned his thoughts to Gray Dove and watched her as she worked below. She had been joined by three other women now.

''Yes, sir,'' he said to himself. ''That's going to be my woman if it takes a hundred horses. That woman is worth a herd of the finest horses this side of old man Mississippi himself, if that's what it takes to measure up to what's expected.''

Chapter 20

Three weeks passed after the hunt and nothing had been said about the test Luke was to take. He felt he had waited long enough and approached Two Feathers.

"About that test you spoke of, I am ready. I am ready for the test. I am ready to go get some horses and most of all I'm ready for a wife. Now, what has to be done to be accepted into the Owl Clan?"

Two Feathers laughed and slapped Luke on the chest. "You are tired of cooking your own meat and want someone to keep a roast on the fire outside of your own tepee?"

"Among other things," Luke responded. "I also need new moccasins." He laughed as he spoke.

"Come, my brother, we will meet with the others and prepare you for your test. We have been waiting for you to ask. You see, we cannot ask you, but you must ask. That is the way."

Luke followed, wondering if he would ever know the ways of the Comanche. There were ways like this that no one would tell him about. One had to stumble into them. Perhaps if he had been raised from a boy with them, he would know. As it was, he had to grasp and struggle to fit within the social structure of the tribe. Gray Dove had been a great help, as had Screaming Hawk. Both had helped him over many obstacles. There were other things he would have to find out by himself.

Two Feathers asked several braves to gather the others and meet him at the edge of camp. In a short time, there were twenty or more young men gathered. "We go now," Two Feathers said.

"Go where?" Luke asked.

"To a sacred place. There we will start, but no one knows where we will end." He looked at a brave close by and both men smiled.

They rode for over an hour and came to a red bluff. There were several large stones protruding from its side. The men dismounted. Two Feathers handed a buffalo robe to Luke.

"You will remove all of your clothes, except your loin cloth. You will take this robe and climb to the top of this bluff. There is a trail, but you must find it. The trail will lead you to the top. There you are to wait until the Great Spirit has talked to you. When you have his message, you will build a fire and burn this robe. We will see the smoke and come back for you. Until you have spoken to the Great Spirit, you are to take nothing to eat or drink. Food and water are forbidden until you have had a vision. If the Great Spirit does not choose to speak to you," he paused, then added, "you could die. If the Great Spirit does not see you to be acceptable, he will not speak to you and you will never belong to any clan. Do you still want to climb to the spot where those of us here have sat before?"

Luke now understood. This was to be a religious experience. "I will climb," he said. "When I see you next, I will have a message from the Great Spirit."

Without a word, the men turned and rode away, leaving Luke alone with only the robe Two Feathers had given him and the moccasins on his feet.

He walked along the bluff and searched for the trail, but was unable to find it. He thought about trying to climb using the large boulders, but decided that would be foolish as the top fifty or sixty feet was sheer and he would be unable to go beyond the stones. He sat down to rest. His mind was searching for a solution and he wondered what he had let himself in for.

"How am I to find a trail if there is none?" he said aloud. As he spoke, he heard a sound. His head snapped around. There stood a deer. It bolted and ran, then disappeared out of sight. Luke followed it. The dusty ground held the hoof prints and led the way. He followed the deer for almost half a mile. He looked up and saw the deer again. It was watching him from the top of the bluff.

Luke followed the deer tracks and found a hidden trail. He had ridden past it when he was led to the spot where Two Feathers had given him the robe. They had passed only a few yards from the trail, yet he had never seen it. He had been looking in the opposite direction. Now he was on the trail. The climb was steep and loose gravel made the climb hard and often very dangerous. At last he reached the top. He looked down. He could see for miles. Never had he realized what a beautiful place this was. In the distance, he could see a cloud bank. It looked like mountains, yet he knew the mountains were many miles away.

"Well, old man deer, you sure showed me the way. Now, if I can just figure out what it is I am supposed to do, I may just make it out of here."

The sun was getting low in the west and dark would soon be at hand. Luke walked to the edge of the bluff. His eyes surveyed the ridge, first to the left then to the right. Something caught his eye that looked out of the ordinary. When he reached the spot, he saw what had caught his attention. There lay the stomach of a buffalo. It appeared to be filled with water. Beside it was a chunk of dried meat. There was a hearth made of stones, wood stacked for a fire, two pieces of flint and a piece of steel. It was apparent that fires had been built here before. Luke spread his robe on the ground.

He tried to recall everything Two Feathers had said. "You must not eat nor drink until you have spoken to the Great Spirit." Those were his words, Luke thought. "I gave my word when I told him I was ready and I'll keep it if it's the last thing I do."

He sat through the night, his mind thinking all kinds of thoughts. He remembered Edward and how he had died. He remembered killing the captain and how scared yet angry he was at the same time. He remembered the war and joining the Army with the hope of a new life. He remembered the day on the plantation when the old master died and how scared he was then.

Luke raised his hands to the sky. The moon had not risen and the stars looked as if they could be touched.

"Oh, Great Spirit," he called out. "I have never come to you before. I never knew how, but now somehow I know that there is no special way. You are there and I am here. You see all, you hear all. You must then know all. I am a poor, dumb soul; but I want to help my new people. Will you show me the way? Will you direct my feet, guide my spear? I need help if I am to do your will. You have spared me from death before. I know I was not meant to die here, alone. Show me the way I am to lead the Comanche to victory.''

Luke waited. The wind blew and dust was stirred up around him. The clouds he had seen earlier were now closing in on him. A storm was in the making. No answer came to him, so he again evoked the Great Spirit and cried out, "Give me a sign. Show me what it is I am to see. Help me.''

A bolt of lightening, followed by a loud clap of thunder, shook the ground. Luke ducked then sat straight up again. He wondered if that was a sign. If it were, he had no idea of what it could mean.

It had now been several hours since he had eaten anything or had a drink of water. He looked at the water bag and thought how good a drink would be, but made no move toward it. Instead he picked up a tiny pebble and placed it in his mouth.

First a drizzle started. It was soon followed by a heavy rain. Luke raised the robe he had been sitting on and held it over his head for protection. The rain let up, but was followed by his worst fear. Hail. The stones bounced all around him. The robe helped to keep the stones from beating him too badly. He hid his body under this flimsy protection and prayed the storm would soon pass. The hailstones grew larger. A gust of wind almost blew the robe off him. Several hailstones hit his body, including his now unprotected head. Luke felt as if he would pass out. His ears rang and his sight seemed to fade.

The storm was over almost as fast as it had come up. Luke pulled the robe back. His head was pounding, his back aching, from the impact of the hailstones. He looked up. The clouds seemed to be getting thinner and, from time to time, he could see a star through a hole in the canopy of gray. He was cold, wet and hungry. He was unable to sleep because of the pain and he sat most of the night with his head resting in his hands. The ground was covered with ice from the storm. He raked a spot clean with his hands. He tried to warm his body with the wet robe.

His mind recalled many things and try as he might, he could not totally remember several things that he tried to recall. Only bits and pieces of his thoughts came together. This caused him to search his memory for those missing parts to the puzzle. In doing this, he was able to induce a state of self-hypnosis even though he was unaware of doing it. He forgot about the pain in his head and the fear that had started to grip him faded.

First light streaked the sky and Luke saw the sun come up. It was then he realized he was truly hurt. His vision was not normal. He was now seeing double. He tried to stand but found his legs did not want to hold his weight. He rose and tried to stretch his legs. He lost his balance and fell. He lay still for a few minutes, then sat up slowly.

"Must have sat too long in one position," he said to himself. "I'll be all right later." He stretched out on his robe. He pulled his legs up to his chest and rubbed them. He stretched out and tried to fall asleep. It was mid-afternoon when he awoke. The sun was high and burned down on him. His lips were swollen and cracked. His tongue felt like it had swollen and filled his mouth. He reached for the water bag. As he did, he thought he heard Two Feathers say, "No water and no food. It is forbidden." He pulled his hand back and looked around. There was only himself and the constant wind blowing across the hilltop, yet it was as if the warning had been spoken. During the storm, he was so cold, now he was burning up. "This must be the test I am to endure."

Night came and a chill came over Luke. He shook so hard he felt every bone in his body would break. During the night, he slept but had dreams that awakened him several times. Once in his dreams, he felt he was falling. Another time, he was being trampled to death by a stampede of horses.

194

He saw the sun rise the second time and he watched the valley below. He saw a doe followed closely by last year's fawn. He watched as they grazed. The doe looked toward where he sat, then returned to grazing. Then her head popped up and she looked back in the direction from which she had come. Luke searched with his eyes, but his sight was still blurred. The double vision had passed, but from time to time, it recurred. When it did, he closed his eyes and rubbed his temples. This seemed to help a little.

Mid-morning he slipped into a deep sleep. It was almost sundown when he awoke. He lay still thinking about what he had seen. He then struggled to sit up. He was weak and dizzy. His thoughts seemed to be confused and he struggled to get control.

"I was there," he said. "I was there. I have been told. I have spoken to the Great Spirit."

With every bone in his body crying out in pain, he crawled to the pile of wood. He pulled from the edge several tiny branches. He twisted the bark off and made his tinder. He struck at the flint with the steel, but missed and hit his thumb. The blood rushed forward and his thumb felt like he had knocked it off his hand. Holding the flint in his palm, he carefully struck the steel to it. Sparks flew, but none caught. He struck the stone several times. The tinder caught a lone spark. He blew, but his breath was weak. The spark faded and went out. He tried again and again. He was not able to catch a spark.

Totally exhausted, he collapsed across the wood and was again in a deep sleep. He awoke during the night and managed to fall back on his robe. He wrapped himself in it to ward off the chill that once again racked his body.

The sun was high and burning down on him when he awakened. He struggled to the wood and again tried to strike the stone. He missed completely. He tried once again and a spark caught. He leaned to blow, but could not manage to reach the spark. A gust of wind blew and stirred up the dust around him. His eyes were still seeing through a haze and the dust that blew into them only made matters worse.

Luke sat back and wiped his eyes, trying to clear his vision. When he opened them, the fire was started. He watched as a glow turned into a flame that started to lick at the smaller limbs. When the blaze was full, he took the robe and laid the edge into the fire. Soon a column of white smoke rose. As the robe burned, the smoke grew more dense. It was then Luke noticed for the first time since he had climbed the bluff that there was no wind, not even a breeze.

He tried to stand but fell backwards and lay there for what seemed forever. He heard voices and opened his eyes. Two Feathers was holding him and trying to help him drink.

"You have had a vision?" he asked

Luke, unable to answer, nodded his head. He tried to smile but his lips were so swollen he could not manage even the slightest of smiles.

Luke was taken back to camp and slept most of the next three days. The second day he felt much better, but was still weak. The bumps on his head had gone down but were still sore to touch. There were several large bruises on his shoulders.

Two Feathers and three braves came into the tepee and sat watching Luke for several minutes.

"Your eyes?" Two Feathers asked. "How do they see?"

He held up his hand and extended one finger. "My eyes are OK. It's what is inside my head that gives me a problem."

"Inside your head? What does this mean?"

Soaring Eagle had entered and took his place next to Two Feathers.

"When I was on the bluff, I fell asleep yet I was awake."

196

Luke sat up and crossed his legs. "I sat like this and tried to talk to the Great Spirit. There was a storm and lightening flashed all around me. I seemed to drift away. When I opened my eyes, I was again standing at a cave much like the one I told you about before. This one was large and guarding the door were two wolves. They were both white. Then a black one came from inside the cave and he ate the first two. He then looked at me and told me to follow him. I did not want to but could not help myself and I followed. As before, inside the dark cave, there was light. I followed the wolf. Again, we came to the snakes. They were much like the other time, but larger. The black wolf jumped at them and they fought. When the fight was over, he had killed the snakes. He told me to have no fear, that he would protect me. He said he was my father and he would not let anything harm me if I would trust him. He then told me to follow him. He led me out into the sunlight. There was my mother again. She stopped me by raising her hands. 'Go back,' she said. 'Your work is not done. You have much to do before you can come to this valley. You are to ride far on a spotted horse with no tail. You are to see many dead buffalo lying on the ground, the sun shining on their bleached bones. You must try to save the buffalo. The buffalo will save your new people.' She then pulled open her blouse and showed her breast. She did not have the breasts of a woman but a large white stripe that ran across where her breasts should have been. 'This is your sign,' she said. 'Your magic.' Then she was gone and I was again on the top of the bluff.

"I knew the Great Spirit had spoken to me through my mother and my father. I knew I had to light the fire. I had to live. The wood was wet and would not burn. I know not how long, but I must have slept again, for when I awoke, I was able to strike a fire and burn the robe. I must somehow save the buffalo from the slaughter I saw. The white stripe on the breast of my mother, I do not understand."

Soaring Eagle raised his hand. "There are those," he said, "who kill many buffalo for the skin. They leave the rest to rot in the sun. These people will kill our brother, the buffalo, and we will starve. We will have no shelter when the cold winds bring the snow. We will be no more unless this is stopped. The white is your mark and if you are to succeed in your task, you must wear this mark when you do battle or you will be lost. The Great Spirit has given you your medicine."

Gray Dove came into the tepee and spoke to Soaring Eagle. "He is still weak and needs his rest." She handed a bowl of broth to No Moon.

"She is right. We go now, my brother," Two Feathers said. "You are now truly Comanche. You have spoken with the Great Spirit. You now belong to the Clan of the Owl."

No Moon lay back down and fell asleep. He rested quietly and did not awake until the following morning. This was the third day after the vision. He sat up and stretched. "I'm so hungry I could eat a horse."

"That might be easy," Gray Dove said, "if you had a horse to eat."

"What is this, woman? Are you saying I don't own a horse?"

"Do you?" she asked.

No Moon rubbed his chin. "Now that you mention it, I guess I don't. The one I've been using belongs to Two Feathers."

Gray Dove left and returned with a large chunk of roast. "This is not horse, but some of the buffalo you killed. I have made a trade for you," she added.

"You made a trade for me?"

"I did. I gave the one called Twisted Foot two of your buffalo skins for a spotted horse. He wanted all three, but

I told him if he did not trade for two, you would speak to your brother, the Moon."

"You did what?"

"You had three skins. The bull, the cow and a calf. I traded the bull and calf skins for a spotted horse. Now you can go with Two Feathers when he goes for horses. He will go when the moon is full. That will be soon." She walked to the opening of the tepee. "You will be strong when he leaves and he will take you with him." She looked down and added, "You need to gather many horses. Two Feathers will show you how."

No Moon took a bite of the roast and just looked at her not speaking. Gray Dove left. He shook his head and thought, "I haven't even asked her to be my wife yet and already she is acting like one. Next thing I know, she will be telling me what I can do and can't do."

The words had not cleared his head when Gray Dove stuck her head back into the tepee and said in a firm voice, "You need to get up and move around. That is the only way you will regain your strength. You cannot sleep in this tepee the rest of your life."

No Moon slapped himself on the head and said, "Get out of my head, woman." There was a warm sound in the tone of his voice as he spoke.

Chapter 21

No Moon rode the spotted horse Gray Dove had traded the hides for. He was surprised to find she had made a good trade for he was a very fine animal. He was large and strong. Since No Moon outweighed most of the Comanche by forty pounds, he needed a larger horse.

There were seven in the party and they rode toward the south for two days then turned east.

"We do not want to go too far that way," Two Feathers said. "The blue coats, ones like you were, are now many. Two days before we left camp, word came that they ride to the west looking for Comanche. They will ride far before they find any." He laughed as he finished talking.

They approached a farm and watched it for almost an hour. They saw a woman and three children as they worked in the garden.

"This is your first raid," Two Feathers said. "You ride

close to me. We will attack and after we have killed them, their hair will fly from our lodge poles. We will take those mules in the pen. Mules make good mounts when we ride in the mountains.'' No Moon knew to draw back now would mean nothing but trouble. Up to this point, he had not really thought of killing women and children, but he knew that was the way of war, Indian as well as white man. If he had to kill, he would, by far, prefer it to be soldiers in a battle. However, for him to be completey Comanche, he knew he must join the others in this raid and kill the woman and children.

''What are we waiting for?'' he asked.

Two Feathers gave a yell and kicked his horse. They raced toward the family below. The woman looked up and screamed. She and the children raced for the house. They dashed in and slammed the door. In no time, shots were fired and one of the braves fell from his horse, mortally wounded with a bullet through the head.

Another rider rode by, leaned over, and grabbed the fallen brave by the arm, lifting him up just as another grabbed his other arm. They rode for cover dragging their dead comrade.

No Moon could hear the hate in Two Feathers' voice as he shouted to the others to kill those in the house. The mules were turned out and ran back toward the hill. Two Feathers set fire to a wagon half filled with hay and with No Moon's help, shoved it next to the house. They then retreated to watch. Soon the house was in full blaze. No one came out. No Moon had seen cabins like that before and knew they probably had a cellar. He did not say anything about it, but said to Two Feathers, ''That is four less whites to bother with.''

Two Feathers nodded, but did not say anything. He kicked his horse and rode to the others who were waiting. They rode off as the cabin was being reduced to ash and smoke.

A chant was held that night and the dead warrior was buried in a small cave. His horse was killed and all of his belongings were placed beside him. The entrance was then filled with rocks and brush.

One of the mules was killed and butchered. After a feast, the men rested. When dawn streaked across the sky, the six of them were riding steadily toward the east.

No Moon asked a brave named Running Dog if there was a special place they were heading. He was told that there was a ranch where they had gathered horses before. It would take two or three more days before they reached it. There were always a great many horses and mules to be had.

There was very little said between the men as they rode. From time to time they changed direction, but always eventually turned back toward the east.

They came to a river and camped for the night. Two Feathers and one of the braves left and were gone for several hours. They returned and told of a town not too far away. There were soldiers in it and it looked like they were planning on staying there. Tents were set up and there were many fires burning around the camp. The land was being cleared and the stockade fence had been started.

Two Feathers knew that with five braves and himself, he would not have a chance for an attack, but he wanted to hit the camp and inflict some damage to it.

"Now is not the time," No Moon said. "Let's go get the horses we came for, then on the way back, we'll just pick up their horses, too."

Two Feathers looked at him and with a sneer on his face, he said, "Now, No Moon, you start to think like a Comanche." They rode most of the night and came to a small stream. They crossed it and waited in a heavy growth of trees while Two Feathers and a brave again rode off, leaving the others to wait. Several hours passed before they returned.

"The Great Spirit has guided us well," Two Feathers said as he rode up. He dismounted and ate a piece of dried meat. He told No Moon and the others that not too far away was a herd of many horses. There were just three riders and they appeared to be only boys. The six left and rode to the grazing herd. It was just as Two Feathers had said. There were over a hundred horses and only three young boys standing guard.

"This is too good to be true," No Moon thought. Why would they leave so many fine horses to be looked after by only three boys? He scouted the surrounding area. He saw nothing that looked out of place. He checked his rifle and sat ready.

Two Feathers gave the signal and they dashed toward the herd. The young boys saw the Indians coming. Two of them turned to ride into the herd. The third raised a rifle to fire, but Two Feathers' spoke first and the boy fell from his mount. They headed the horses down the draw and out over a hill. Somehow they managed to gain control and kept the herd together. They rode hard for several hours. The herd tired and slowed to a steady trot, then to a walk.

No Moon rode to the front where Two Feathers had stationed himself. "They'll be coming after us. You know that, don't you?" he asked.

"They will. Yes, I know that. When we reach the river, we will change and go north toward the big river. We will split and go three different ways. That way, they will follow only one group. The other two will be free to move back to the canyon with no problem."

"What about the soldiers?" No Moon asked.

Two Feathers smiled. "We will come back for them with more braves and rid that valley of them."

When they reached the river, No Moon and a young brave took about one-third of the herd and headed straight for home. The rest of the herd was divided. One group swung north, the other southwest.

After three days, the young brave with No Moon pointed toward a canyon. "We wait there," he said. "Wait? Two Feathers did not say anything about waiting."

"We wait there. Soon the others will join us." His voice convinced No Moon that he knew what he was talking about.

They drove the herd into what turned out to be a box canyon. They closed the mouth with brush and ropes, then stationed themselves on both sides at the top of the canyon.

It was late afternoon the next day when Bent Bow called to No Moon. "There," he shouted and pointed to a dust cloud on the horizon.

"You tell me when they are near," Bent Bow shouted. "I will open the canyon."

No Moon watched the herd as it approached. He waved at Bent Bow and he began to drag the brush from the opening. The horses inside became restless as the herd neared. Running Dog brought his herd into the canyon with no problem. The four men now rejoiced at their meeting. The brush was returned and they again went to the hilltop to watch for Two Feathers.

When morning came, Running Dog approached No Moon. "He should have been here by now. If he does not come by dark, we must take the horses and leave at first light."

"What could have happened to him?"

"Maybe the one whose horses we took caught him and Gray Wolf. We may never know if he does not come."

No Moon strained his eyes to see a dust cloud, but none was to be seen. He sat watching until he could no longer see because of the darkness. As he sat by the small fire with the others, he spoke looking at the flames as they licked at the burning log. "I'm not going to leave until I know what happened. You three can lead the herd back to the village. I've got to find out what has happened to my friend."

He looked at each brave. No one spoke. They knew No Moon was a man of his word.

Chapter 22

No Moon watched as the three braves started the herd on the trail home. He saw them go over the ridge and only then did he pull his horse's head around and start back to the place where only a few days ago he had seen the beginnings of a fort. He rode hard.

He thought to himself, "If Two Feathers is alive, I've got to try to save him. Without him I would have trouble gaining the leadership I need. Chances are if he has been caught, it would have been by a patrol. The only place a patrol could have come from between here and the place where we got the horses would be that new fort we saw."

He put his horse into a trot. "Well, old boy, I think we'll go check that place out."

Keeping to the low valleys and brushy areas, No Moon made his way back toward the new fort. If Two Feathers was alive and was, indeed, a prisoner, he would be held at the fort. The last thing No Moon wanted was to be seen by anyone that could alert the soldiers stationed there.

No Moon tied his horse to a small bush in a wide arroyo with a thick growth of trees and brush. He was still a good half mile away from the fort, but decided it would be safer to go on foot than to risk the chance of being seen.

He lay in the brush on top of a small rise which gave him a good vantage point. The soldiers were going about their work. He was surprised and pleased to see that the enlisted men who were working were black.

"Must be one of those infantry groups I heard about. Not enough horses to be a mounted outfit," he said to himself.

He stayed at his vantage point for several hours. Then to his surprise, he saw an Indian as he was led out of a tent. He was taken to a post and chained. The guards left. There was only one left to watch over the prisoner. He watched for several minutes. He felt sure the Indian was Two Feathers, but he could not be certain. As luck would have it, three soldiers headed out of a corral with a small herd of horses. They were taking them out for grazing. Two Feathers' horse was in the herd.

"That's him," he said aloud. "Got to get in. But how?" He looked at the buckskins he wore. He saw a sergeant come out of a tent. His chevron shone bright on his arm. He walked across what would soon be the parade field and went into another, smaller tent. Several minutes passed and he stepped outside. His shirt was off and he pitched out a pan of water.

"Well, well, well, Sergeant, hope you don't mind if I borrow your uniform tonight," he whispered.

It was after dark and No Moon listened as taps were blown on the bugle. The flag had been lowered and he remembered how excited he was when he first joined the Army. That seemed ages ago now, but the feeling of excitement still ran through his veins. Several of the fires died out. He watched as the sentries walked their posts.

Two Feathers was still chained to the post. He had not been given food or water.

"They would whip the daylights out of a trooper if he treated a horse like that. But an Indian..." His thoughts changed to the sergeant he had seen earlier. The lamp in his tent was now out.

With great care, No Moon crept closer. He waited until a guard passed close by. He sprang from the dark and grabbed the guard. He brought down his war club hard on his head. The guard slumped to the ground. He drug him into some brush, then moving slowly he crept to the edge of the sergeant's tent. He listened. He could hear snoring. Slowly he entered. He stepped on the saber lying at the foot of the bunk. The sergeant sat up in bed.

"Who's there?" he said.

No Moon brought his club down on the sergeant's head. The sergeant slumped back in the bed, then rolled to the ground. He moaned, then lay silent.

No Moon found the sergeant's uniform in the dark and put it on. He then walked straight to the guard watching over Two Feathers.

"Unchain him," he ordered.

"Who are you?" the guard asked.

"Sergeant Luke Gray. Now unchain this man. The captain wants to see him."

Two Feathers opened his eyes. He wanted to shout, but knew better. He watched as No Moon took charge and played the role of a soldier.

"Look here, Sergeant, I ain't gonna unchain him until Sergeant Wells tells me to."

"Soldier, you unchain that devil right now or so help me, you'll find yourself standing right along beside him when we hang him."

"You don't have to go and get all upset about it. I was only doing what I was told." As the soldier spoke, he unchained Two Feathers. "You don't mind if I go with you, do you, Sergeant?"

"Wouldn't have it any other way," he answered.

The three of them headed for the main tent. No Moon stopped and said, "Got to get a report from my tent." He turned back toward the tent where he had taken the uniform. The private followed with Two Feathers between them. He went inside the tent and called out, "Private, come here, will you?"

The private stuck his head inside. It was met with a war club. No Moon then reached out and drug Two Feathers inside. Using the keys he found in the pocket of the sergeant's uniform, he removed the chains and whispered, "Follow me." The two men crept to the corral where the horses were kept. No Moon motioned for Two Feathers to stop and he approached the guard. "Halt," came the charge. He stopped.

"Who goes there?"

"Jesus Christ," No Moon answered.

"Who?"

"Jesus Christ. What's the matter, boy? Ain't you never heard of old Sergeant Luke Gray, better known as Jesus Christ?"

"What kind of trash you saying, Sergeant?" the young guard responded. "I don't even know . . ." He never finished his statement. Two Feathers brought No Moon's club down on the guard's head.

They opened the gate to the corral. Each selected a mount and together they gave a scream and kicked the horses they were on. The entire remuda followed. Twenty-two horses and as many mules ran through the camp. Shouts could be heard and several shots were fired, but No Moon and Two Feathers were safely out of range and lost in the dark to those who would have shot them.

The two of them laughed and shouted as they rode toward the setting moon. When daylight came, they had put many miles between them and the soldiers. They rested and No Moon was glad to see that his spotted horse had broken free and followed the herd. He caught the mount and held him close patting him on the chest.

"This is my medicine," he said. "Gray Dove traded and this horse filled the vision. I will never give him up. If he had not followed us, I would have had to go back for him."

Two Feathers chuckled. "You lose that horse, you had better not show up for a long time. Gray Dove argued with old Twisted Foot half a day before he gave in to her trade."

"Well," No Moon said as they rested. "We aren't going back empty handed. We've got maybe fifty or sixty horses we captured from the ranch and these right here, plus one Comanche brave." He pointed at Two Feathers.

Two Feathers laughed. "The best part you leave for last." He pitched a stone at No Moon.

"Now we will talk marriage when we get back," No Moon remarked. "I'll offer Soaring Eagle ten horses and a Comanche."

"The horses he will take, the Comanche even he sometimes wonders about." Both men laughed and dozed off.

Chapter 23

The moon came up early. It was full and the orange glow filled the horizon. No Moon sat with Two Feathers and the rest of his clan. They awaited the signal that was to be given by Soaring Eagle. Luke's eyes were fixed on the opening of the tepee of Gray Dove's parents. Finally the old man stepped out. He folded his arms and looked around. He acted as if nothing was going on.

"Now," Two Feathers said in a low voice.

No Moon rose to his feet and walked toward Soaring Eagle. He was followed by a brave who led three horses. He stopped three or four feet from Soaring Eagle. The two men stood in silence. No Moon motioned for the brave to hand Soaring Eagle the lead ropes to the horses.

"I come to you," No Moon said, "as an outsider. I give to you this many horses," he held up his right hand showing all five fingers, "for each horse that is here. In return, I would take Gray Dove to be my woman.''

Soaring Eagle did not speak, but stared, unblinking, at No Moon.

His mind raced trying to remember what else he had been instructed to say by Two Feathers. He glanced in Two Feathers' direction. Two Feathers used his thumb and pointed at his chest. This gave him the signal and his memory was jogged.

"I, No Moon," he continued, "have long sought your daughter for my woman. I have proven myself in battle. I have spoken with the Great Spirit and have been accepted into the Clan of the Owl. This token I have given to you shows that I can provide for your daughter, Gray Dove." He paused. "Will you accept my token?"

Soaring Eagle stood without moving for what seemed forever. Then a smile crossed his normally solemn face. His eyes seemed to twinkle and he reached out and took the lead ropes. He did not say a word.

A great sound filled the camp. All of the men gave out with their shouts. The women joined in.

Gray Dove came out of the tepee. She was dressed in a white doeskin dress. The beadwork covering the front was a work of art. The fringe on each sleeve hung from her elbow to her hand. The skirt had also been fringed from mid-calf to the top of her matching moccasins. When she approached No Moon, he saw a beauty he had never seen before. Gray Dove's pitch black hair glistened in the light.

He took a deep breath. He felt his heart start to bound. The pulse in his throat felt as though his neck would pop open.

Two Feathers had now approached and was standing next to his father. Gray Dove stood between them. All three faced No Moon. Soaring Eagle extended his hand, palm up. Two Feathers laid the ceremonial knife, which was a long slender flint blade with a carved deer horn handle, in his father's hand.

"Give me your left hand," Soaring Eagle said.

No Moon extended his hand. As he did, it was met by the left hand of Gray Dove. Soaring Eagle cut a small gash in each palm and using his free hand joined the two hands together.

"Your blood now flows together. Each will have his mate's blood flow through his heart. You are as one." His voice seemed to quiver for a second. Then in the voice of a once strong, brave man, he proclaimed, "Gray Dove is now the woman of the man we call No Moon."

A cheer went up. Several of the young braves formed a circle and danced around the central fire. After they had made three complete circles, they were joined by a like number of young women forming a circle inside the men's circle. They danced in different directions.

"The rest of the night there will be dancing and songs," Gray Dove said.

"I hope they don't plan on us sticking around for the whole party," No Moon commented.

Gray Dove smiled and in a girlish manner lowered her head to speak. "No. We are to slip away and spend the night in the woods. Or if you want, in your tepee. But in your tepee, we will be called on by your friends. They will stay the night and talk about old times. I will be left alone to sleep by myself."

No Moon, with a serious expression on his face, shook his head and said, "You've got about as much chance of being alone as you do of eating snow in the summer." He looked around and saw the women starting to lay out chunks of meat that had been cooking. Several people had already begun to eat.

"Now's the time," he thought. He took Gray Dove to his

tepee and they went in. He dropped the door flap. Holding Gray Dove's hand, he went straight to the opposite side of the tent and raised the bottom. She knew what to do and slid under. "They can come calling," No Moon said, "but nobody is going to be at home."

From the hilltop where they spent the night, the view was breathtaking during the day. Miles of the valley below could be seen. At night it took on an entirely different appearance. The ripples in the surface of the stream below sparkled like a million fireflies. The full moon lit up the entire valley and gave the night a softness only two young people deeply in love could really appreciate.

No Moon spread the buffalo robe he had brought. He pulled Gray Dove close to him and kissed her. Every fiber in his body wanted to shout with the happiness he now felt. Neither said a word, but thoughts were being transmitted between the two of them.

After several minutes, No Moon said in a quiet voice, "Once long ago on a night much like this one, I dreamed of being as happy as I am tonight. I never told anyone because I could not see how this could ever happen. Never did I expect that dream to come true, but here I am." He rolled over and looked at Gray Dove. "No man could be happier than I am right now."

Gray Dove smiled. She, too, was filled with happiness on this night of her marriage.

It was early when No Moon awoke. He sat up and looked around. He was alone. Gray Dove was nowhere to be seen. He looked down the trail and could see her coming back up the hillside. She was carrying something in a blanket.

"Would you look at that," he said. "She went back to camp and gathered up some food for us." As he watched her, he noticed the brush moving next to the trail. He realized the danger and tried to shout. The wind had started to blow

216

and his voice was lost.

Gray Dove, unaware of the danger, was headed straight to where three men were hiding in the brush next to the trail. No Moon, armed only with a settler's butcher knife he had taken in a raid, ran down the trail toward Gray Dove. His shouts were heard just as she reached the ambush. The three men jumped out and grabbed her. Her strength was unbelievable. She kicked out and caught one of the would-be attackers in the chest sending him backwards. He fell over a dead log. No Moon had now reached the site. He dove from a ledge over the trail and crashed down on top of one of the men. His knife was driven deep into the fallen man's ribs. He rolled and bounced to his feet. The third man now had his left arm around Gray Dove's neck. His right hand held a knife to her chest.

"Apache dog!" Gray Dove shouted. As she did she brought her foot down with a crushing blow to her captor's instep. He drew back with his knife. It was fast, but there was enough time for No Moon to move. He rushed in and delivered a smashing blow to the face of the Apache. The blade flashed. It caught him with a glancing blow in the arm and stopped what would have been a death blow to Gray Dove. She fell to the ground. No Moon moved in unaware of his injury. His weight carried the two men to the ground and they rolled down the sloping trail, locked in mortal combat.

No Moon knew he had to free his knife hand. He saw an opening and smashed his head into the face of the Apache. The Apache released his grip and No Moon drove his knife blade deep into the bronze body. He pulled the blade free and drove it in again. The Apache now lay limp beside the trail.

No Moon regained his footing and started back up the trail when he saw the Indian Gray Dove had kicked start to get up. Gray Dove brought a stick down on his head. He grunted and sank to his knees. She hit him again and he fell face forward in the dirt.

"You are hurt!" Gray Dove shouted as she grabbed No Moon's arm.

"I'm OK, I'm OK," he said. "Are you hurt?"

"I am mad," she said. "These dogs used to do this all the time until Soaring Eagle ran them away. Now, they have returned." As she spoke, she looked at his wound. "You are lucky. Your cut is not bad." She tore a strip from the blanket she had been carrying and wrapped it around his arm.

He rolled the Apache over that Gray Dove had hit. "These are scouts. These three are Army scouts. Go get Two Feathers. We've got to get this one awake and find out where they came from."

Gray Dove ran back to camp. It was only a short time before Two Feathers and several other braves returned. The Apache scout had started to come around. No Moon had tied his hands behind his back. Two Feathers grabbed the scout and placed his knife next to the man's throat.

"Don't kill him. We need to find out if there are any more and where they came from." Two Feathers released the scout's hair. No Moon reached down and grabbed him.

"Where did you come from?" he demanded.

The Apache spit at him. No Moon's hand flew through the air and caught the scout squarely on the jaw sending him sprawling backwards. No Moon followed him down and straddled the scout and holding him by the hair asked him, "Do you speak English?" There was no response, only hate in the stare he received. Then in Spanish, he asked him, "Habla espanol?"

"Si," was the response.

"Good." He released the man's hair and speaking in Spanish said, "You know you are a dead man. What you can do is die fast or slow. It all depends on what you want.

218

The Comanche can make you die for days. I can tie a rope around your neck and keep the spirit in your body forever. It all depends on you. You understand?"

"I understand, black one."

No Moon was still sitting on the scout's chest. "What are you doing here? Are you scouts for the Army?"

"We scout for Mackenzie."

"Mackenzie? Impossible. He's back in San Antonio."

"He is here on staked plains. He is looking for Comanches. He is looking for black Comanche. It is you who will have his spirit locked inside of him forever when he finds you."

No Moon stood up and looked down. "How many of you came to this place?"

The Apache smiled and with a sneer said, "You will find out soon, black one."

Without looking around, No Moon asked for a rope. He was handed a braided rawhide lariat. He bent down and slid the loop over the Apache's head and tightened the loop. "Let's find a good strong limb," he said as he grabbed the scout by the arm and pulled him to his feet.

The Apache tried to twist free, but his effort was wasted. He was dragged to a nearby tree. No Moon tossed the loose end of the lariat over a low limb. He pulled the rope tight. "Make your peace, dog, because your spirit will never leave this spot." He gave the rope a jerk, then released it.

The Apache coughed and sank to his knees. "If I tell you what you want to know, you give me your word, the word of the Comanche, I will not die with the spirit locked inside of me?"

"My word is given." As No Moon spoke, he slapped his chest with his right hand.

"We three ran away from the Army. We go back to the mountains in the south. We go to the place called Mexico. We saw woman. We wanted woman to go with us. We do

219

not want war with Comanche.''

"Is the Army close to this place?" No Moon asked.

"No. Maybe five, six suns to east. They built a new fort there. When it is completed, many blue coats with long knives will come and kill all Comanche.''

"And you would help them, wouldn't you?"

There was no answer.

"You fool, don't you know the white man is using Indians to kill Indians. He can't find them so he gets dogs like you to hunt his own kind down. Your kind is the worst of all enemies.''

The scout had now risen to his feet and stood facing No Moon and Two Feathers. "When the Comanche is dead, the Apache will kill all of the white ones. Then we will have all of our land back again.''

"You fool." As No Moon spoke, he drove his knife deep into the heart of the scout. "Get these dogs out of here," he ordered. "Take them out on the flat land and let the coyotes and buzzards feast on their flesh." He turned to Two Feathers. "We need to send men out in all directions and see if what he said was the truth. If there are soldiers near, we need to do what has to be done. If it's battle, then we will fight. If we are lucky, he was not telling the truth. I have heard of the one called Mackenzie. He is bad medicine.''

Three days passed and the scouting parties returned. The Apache had been telling the truth. No Moon was met by Gray Dove as he rode into camp. He was leading four horses and a mule. He dismounted and they embraced.

"Where did you get those?" she asked.

"Ran across a couple hide hunters yesterday. We talked for a while and when I left, they didn't need this stock any more, so I just brought it back with me. I hate to see good stock go unused.''

220

Chapter 24

Almost a year had passed since No Moon had taken Gray Dove for his wife. He had been on several raids. His herd had grown and by Indian standards, he was rich. Very rich. Yet he felt he had not yet done or even begun to do what he was supposed to do.

He and several other braves were breaking horses when a rider came into camp. He reported having seen many buffalo to the north. They were making their migration early this year.

"It is going to be a cold winter," No Moon remarked. "If they are moving south this early, they feel the snows coming."

"You may be right," Two Feathers remarked. "Then maybe something else is driving them to the winter range early."

"Like what?"

"Hunters. Maybe Blackfoot, maybe even Apache or Cheyenne. They could hunt hard and push them this way early."

Two Feathers then looked north. "There have been reported in the past great fires that sweep the grasslands for many days. If this happens the buffalo must flee for his life. There are many reasons why he is early."

No Moon nodded. "You are probably right, but I say it's going to be an early and cold winter."

The two men looked at each other, then No Moon added, "Really doesn't matter. The buffalo are here and it is time to hunt."

"It is time to hunt!" Two Feathers shouted. "We go tomorrow." A cheer went up among the braves.

As with every other major hunt in which No Moon had participated, and there had been four, the men left first and were followed by the women and a few selected braves. Some of the women, the very small children and the old ones stayed in camp. Each had their job and without question, they went about their assigned tasks. When it came to the hunt, everyone knew his job and no one needed to tell even the youngest child what had to be done.

It took two days of hard riding to get to the place where the buffalo were said to be. The great plains stretched for miles and served as a natural graze-way for the beasts as they migrated to their winter range. The plains were dotted with small shallow lakes and water was usually easy to find. Over the years, with perhaps millions of buffalo using these lakes, they had deepened and widened because of the sharp hooves trampling back and forth in the annual migration of the animals. No Moon and Two Feathers were out in front when they topped a small ridge. Off in the distance, they saw what looked like a thousand black spots in the sky. "Look at that."

Two Feathers strained his eyes. Never had he seen

anything like it before.

"Those are buzzards. But why so many?" he asked, not to No Moon but to himself.

"Buzzards? Are you sure?"

"I am sure." As he spoke, he nudged his pony over the rim and put him into a trot. No Moon followed.

They rode for almost an hour. No Moon sniffed. He smelled something, but could not identify the odor. They crossed a gully and rode up a small knoll. There in a basin as far as they could see lay dead buffalo rotting in the sun.

No Moon could not believe his eyes. "There must be seven or eight hundred. Maybe more." Two Feathers did not respond, but nudged his pony forward. He rode around the dead animals. No Moon followed. Each animal had been skinned, the carcass left to rot.

Two Feathers stopped and looked down at a wagon trail. He said, "The white man has found our brother. They have come with the heart of an evil spirit. They kill the buffalo and take only the hide. They leave the rest to rot and fill the bellies of the buzzards. This is their trail. We will follow it and when we find them, we will punish them. We will kill every one of them and they will never again do this thing to us. We will leave them to rot and feed the buzzards. Their bodies will be blackened from the sun, just as the buffalo have been."

They rode back and met the others who had waited on the knoll while No Moon and Two Feathers rode among the dead buffalo.

"We will find those who did this," Two Feathers said to his braves, "and they will die. You," he pointed to a young brave, "will go back and tell the others to turn back and return to the village. There will be no hunt. Our lodges will be hungry when the snows fly. Twisted Foot, you will take your clan and go to the west. Perhaps part of the great herd scattered and went that way. If you find them, send word.

The rest of us will track the hide hunters.''

Once he had given his instructions, Two Feathers pulled his horse's head around and trotted back to the wagon tracks.

They followed the tracks for the rest of the afternoon. At dark, camp was made in a clump of cottonwoods and the horses were rested. Two scouts went out after the moon had risen. The moon was almost full and lit the prairie well enough to see. The wagons had mashed down the tall grass and the trail was no problem to follow.

Before daylight, the scouts returned and told Two Feathers that at the next stream camped in a cottonwood thicket were four white men, two Mexican women and a young boy. ''The wagons are filled with hides from the buffalo.''

Two Feathers jumped to his pony, raised his lance and shouted. Followed by all the braves, he headed for the hide hunters' camp.

The camp was located at the foot of a small bluff. The water in the creek was shallow and since the rainy season had not started, the current was just a trickle.

Using hand signals, Two Feathers divided the group into thirds. Two of the parties would move in opposite directions and cut off any escape route. The third and largest party would lie in wait and would attack head-on when the others were in position.

No Moon had taken one of the parties that was to block the exits. The horses were left a safe distance away and they moved in on foot. Since the prairie grass was almost waist high, they were able to move in very close.

No Moon saw a very large man with long, shaggy hair approach the young boy as he sat scraping a hide. The man without warning struck out and hit the boy with his open hand. The lad was knocked over backwards and lay curled up on the ground to protect himself. The man stood over him and shouted. No Moon's Spanish was not the best, but it had improved over the years. Spanish was always used when trading with other tribes and the comancheros.

He heard the man say, "You cut another hide, I'll cut your hide. You ain't worth the powder it would take to blow you to hell anyway."

One of the two women helped the boy up and took him to the creek bank where she washed the blood from his face.

"You there, woman," the big man shouted, "get over here! You ain't got time to fool with that hunk of trash."

The woman did as she was told and went back to the hide she had been scraping. The big man said something No Moon did not understand and shoved one of the other men in a playful act. They both laughed. The big man moved to the two women who were working. He reached down and grabbed one of them by the hair and pulled her to her feet. She tried to strike him, but her arm was caught in his strong grip. He slapped her face and said something about her talking too much and all he wanted to see or hear was her scraping hides.

No Moon could watch no more. He cocked his rifle and drew a bead. He squeezed the trigger and his rifle spoke the tune of death. The big man straightened up with a surprised look on his face, then fell backwards. No Moon had shot him through the neck just below the jaw.

When No Moon shot, it was if a signal had been given. Two Feathers, followed by fifteen braves, stormed the camp. The fight was over in just a few minutes. The hide hunters were all dead. The two women and the boy huddled together knowing that they, too, would die. One of the braves grabbed a woman and pulled her aside. "This one belongs to me," he shouted. Another brave made a move toward the second woman, the one the big man had slapped.

"That one is for me!" No Moon shouted.

Another brave looked at No Moon and smiled, "This one

225

for me," he said. "This one is my woman."

No Moon stepped past the woman and looked down at the Indian. He was a good fifty pounds heavier and a foot taller. "I said this one is mine." His voice was stern. "You touch her and I'll rip out your tongue, then feed it to the coyotes."

The Indian withdrew, but not before making a threatening gesture with his finger across his throat.

"You have made an enemy," Two Feathers said.

"You are wrong. He has made an enemy. I've got me a woman to carry wood. Gray Dove is with child and she needs help. I claim this one for my tepee." Two Feathers grunted his approval.

"We may not have a lot of meat this winter, but we will have a lot of hides for robes and tepees. We have killed those who would kill our buffalo, but they have left us all of these hides. With the three wagons they used, we also have twelve mules to pull the hides to our village. The three horses should go to Two Feathers for leading us here. Back at our village, we will divide all of these hides. We will make many robes. Those left over, we use in trade with the Mexican who sometimes comes."

No Moon looked at Two Feathers. "That sound fair to you?"

"Can you put the mules in this?" Two Feathers asked as he held up a set of traces.

No Moon smiled. "Cut my teeth on those," he chuckled.

He had the harness in place quickly. Using the women and boy as drivers, the group headed back toward the village. Two Feathers rode up to No Moon who was riding next to a wagon driven by the woman he claimed.

"Why did you shoot the big one?"

No Moon looked at the woman, then back at Two Feathers. "I just felt he needed shooting."

226

Chapter 25

The wind turned cold. It blew day and night for almost a week. First came the drizzle, then the temperature dropped and the first flurries of snow drifted down into the canyon. No Moon had been right. Winter had come early and, from its first blast, it was to be a very cold one.

He had been leading scouts out on the prairie the same as Two Feathers. He was functioning as a sub-chief and his hunting skills had proven to be very good. His last scouting trip had taken his party into New Mexico and they were able to bring back several deer and a bear.

There would be food this winter, but everyone would have to take part to conserve. There would be no feast, but the chances were that no one would die from lack of food. They all knew that before spring, they would be eating horses to survive.

The last hunt No Moon had been on had been good, but

the hunters had to travel a great distance. He was tired and, from time to time after a long ride, the old wound in his side would hurt. It hurt now as he crouched close to a small fire. Four of his braves sat with him as he waited and watched his tepee.

Gray Dove was in heavy labor inside the tepee. She was aided by two midwives. One was the Mexican he had claimed from the buffalo hunters. Her name was Lupe. From time to time, he could hear a whimper come from inside. He knew Gray Dove was in pain. He had seen birthing before back on the plantation. He knew of the pain that accompanied that feature of nature.

No Moon tossed a stick on the flame. The coals sent embers up in a small cloud of smoke. One of the braves sitting close to the fire had a spark fall on the inside of his bare leg where his leather leggings gapped open. He gave a yell and fell backwards slapping at the burn. This was treated as a joke and the men laughed, including the one who was burned.

First came a slight whimper. No Moon sat up and listened closely. A scream was followed by the crying of a baby. Lupe stuck her head out of the tepee and motioned for him to come. Somehow he had a feeling he had not had for a very long time. Fear grabbed his inner soul. Yet there was a feeling of happiness, excitement and pride. He knew he had fathered a child.

"I hope it's a boy, but if it is a girl I will not show my disappointment," he said to himself.

Slowly he entered the tepee. Gray Dove lay on the buffalo robe with a baby in her arms. He brushed the hair from the side of her face. Reaching down, he gently touched the baby and looked at Gray Dove. He lifted the doe skin covering the baby and saw it was a boy.

"You have a son," Gray Dove said. She no sooner said

the words when her face showed great pain. She grunted and flinched.

Lupe took the baby and shoved No Moon out of the opening. "You stay," she said. "No place for man."

No Moon did not have any idea what was going on. He stood there wondering what he was supposed to do. His wait was short. A new voice cracked the stillness of that cold winter day. He pulled back the entrance flap and looked inside. Gray Dove now held two babies. Pride swelled up and he gave a great war whoop. He turned to his braves still sitting by the fire. Holding up two fingers, he said, "Gray Dove has given me two." He stopped and turned back to the tepee. "Lupe!" he shouted. "Is the second one a boy?"

"Si," came the reply.

"Two boys!" he said to his friend. "Not one, but two Comanches are now in the tepee of No Moon." He did a short dance around the fire and his friends laughed at this proud father. He did not know that not too many years before, one of the twins would have been killed. Now even this old custom had changed.

With the babies born, things returned to normal. Gray Dove was up and moving before dark. She was the one who cooked the night meal. Lupe took charge of the newborn boys.

No Moon and Two Feathers discussed another horse raid. They were selecting who would ride. They did not like to go out on these raids with a large group. That made them more vulnerable and easier to detect. A small party of four or five could move fast. They could get in and get out before the owners of the horses even knew they were around.

"Horse With Short Tail is still mad about me keeping Lupe, isn't he?" No Moon asked. Two Feathers nodded in agreement.

"You think I'll eventually have trouble with him?"

"Some day he will try to get even." Two Feathers looked across the camp at Horse With Short Tail's tepee. He tossed his head in that direction. "He will wait until he thinks you have forgotten, then he will make his move. Maybe not at you, but at something you own. Maybe some day even one of your sons."

No Moon slid his knife from its sheath and touched the blade with his thumb. "That would be a mistake." He looked at the tepee across the camp. "It might be better if I just called him out and got this thing done with here and now. How many big hunts have I been on now? Four or five? He could have gone on any of them and taken a chance of killing me then, but he chose to go with you or some other hunt chief."

Two Feathers sat in silence and watched the tepee. After several minutes, he said, "It would be bad for you to provoke a fight. It would be the smart thing to do, but the results would be bad. You took the woman and he had nothing. Now, if you kill him, there are those who will say you still have the greed of the white man in you. They will think that you will kill anybody who gives you trouble. No, my brother, it would serve you no good to kill him, unless he makes a move against you. Then you had better kill him or he will kill you."

Horse With Short Tail came out of his tepee. He stood up and looked in the direction of No Moon and Two Feathers. He turned and said something to someone inside, then looked back. He started walking toward the two men. Horse With Short Tail stopped and speaking to Two Feathers, he said, "You look a hole through my tepee."

Two Feathers stood up and smiled as he spoke. "The hole in your tepee is caused because you do not take care of it."

"Why do you sit here with him and look my way? Do you plan on doing something to Horse With Short Tail?"

"We plan nothing except a hunt. Would you ride with No Moon?"

The young brave turned and looked at No Moon. "I ride as Comanche. Matters not to me who is hunt chief."

"Good. Parties will ride tomorrow. You will ride with my brother here."

Horse With Short Tail grumbled and walked away without saying a word.

"Think he will?"

"He will," Two Feathers answered.

As Two Feathers had said, they rode out in search of game as planned. No Moon's scouting party rode to the West and searched for four days without a trace of any game. Half frozen, they turned back empty-handed and returned to the canyon.

"There will be many horses eaten this year," one of the braves said.

"Better to eat the horses than to chew on old buffalo hides," another said.

When they met Two Feathers back in the camp, they were not surprised to find that his hunt went no better than their own. The plains were void of game. The young brave was right. There would be many horses eaten this winter.

Two Feathers asked how it went with Horse With Short Tail. No Moon rubbed his head and told Two Feathers that Horse With Short Tail did not say two words on the entire scout. When he had something to say, he spoke to one of the other braves and then only with hand signals.

"You watch that one. He is not done with his hate. He will try to get even when he can pick the time."

"When that time comes, he will have seen his last sunrise. If I had known this hate would run so deep, I may have given him the woman. But now I cannot."

The winter passed and the snow melted and ran away into

231

the stream located in the bottom of the canyon. No Moon had talked long and hard during the winter to the elders and Two Feathers. When spring came, he would start his training of the Indians. If they were to win the war that would surely come, they had to fight the white man's way. They would, however, also include many of the Comanche ways.

"The blending of the two will make us victorious," he had promised. "Weapons and ammunition is what we need most. Where are these things? They are at the army forts. We will take them the same as when I came for you when you were held prisoner," he had told Two Feathers.

Spring was starting to renew life around them. The time to start was at hand. They could wait no longer.

For several weeks No Moon worked with the young braves. There were parts of the training that went well, but there were parts that crumbled in disaster. Holding a straight line in formation seemed to be lost every time the horses started to move. Each brave wanted to ride at his pace and be close to his personal friends. After talking to Two Feathers, it was decided to work only on the plan of attack. Any attempt at a formation would have to be forgotten. Besides, Two Feathers could see no reason for a formation. The battle was all that accounted for the final results, not how nice the braves lined up.

The most important thing was, of course, how to wage a successful attack. After all, the Comanches had been riding to battle since the first Comanche caught his first horse. Nowhere on the plains was there a more skilled and competent rider than the Comanche warrior. No Moon knew this and agreed to forego all but the attack plan.

A mock battle was staged and the flanks were explained time and time again. No Moon and Two Feathers sat on their horses and No Moon blew the call for attack on a bugle one of the young Indians had given him. The bugle was no doubt taken from a fallen soldier in one of their encounters. He moved one flank in, then the full thrust of the front line. He blew retreat and signaled for the remaining flank to close in. He sounded a recall and the entire body moved in on the mock target in Indian style.

Just what he had been afraid of happened. With shouts and war cries, they started to form a circle around the target. In the fashion of battle they had always fought, they rode in squeezing the circle smaller as they rode. No Moon blew his bugle. It went unnoticed. He blew again and again. There was no response.

"For crying out loud!" No Moon shouted in English. He fired his rifle into the air. The shot caused the circle to break up and Comanche braves rode in all directions and headed back to No Moon and Two Feathers.

"It will never work," Two Feathers said.

"It's got to work." As he spoke, No Moon turned to face Two Feathers. As many of his plans had before, an idea came in a flash as if a picture was shown to him. The idea could be the key he was looking for. He just might get the importance of the new way to fight over to every brave in the tribe.

The braves now sat on their horses laughing and talking about the way they had ridden in on the target. Each thought he had performed admirably in the finest tradition of a Comanche warrior.

"Get down off your horses," No Moon ordered.

A look of disbelief crossed Two Feathers' face. He knew the men would not dismount just because No Moon told them to.

"If you want to live as you always have, then do as you always have. Maybe you will last two or three, maybe even five, winters more." He paused and looked at the silent faces watching him. "Then, my friends, we will all be gone. We will be no more. Our bones will bleach in the sun just as the buffaloes' now do. If you want your sons to be Comanche braves and his sons to know this land as we know it, let me show you the way." No Moon pointed to the sky. "I have spoken to the Great Spirit and he has shown me the way. Now I must show you." He paused again, then shouted, "Get off your horses!"

Two Feathers slid off his paint and stood by its side. Several others followed. Slowly every brave dismounted. Only No Moon was still sitting atop his mount. "Hear me, my brothers. I make a pledge to you here and now. You do what I say and fight the way I show you. If you do not win a major battle against the white soldiers, then I will leave never to return. But when we beat them into the ground, and we will, you must give me your word as Comanche braves that you will follow whoever is the war chief and fight only his battle, not the battle of your fathers." He looked around.

One of the braves shouted, "It has always been so!"

No Moon picked up on the statement. "It has always been so?" he asked.

"Yes. We have fought our way for many years and we control all we want. No other red man can claim such victories as the Comanche."

A cheer went up. When the braves were again quiet, No Moon said, "Suppose all of your horses were killed in that valley below and you had not one single horse left."

Two Feathers said, "We cannot fight without horses. It is the horse that carries us on the warpath. It is the horse that helps us take the game we need to feed the tribe."

"That is the point, my brother. The Comanche has not always had the horse. You know that as well as I. So you see, it has not always been so. You have learned to war on horseback instead of on foot. Now, learn how to war even better on horseback, like the white man and the black

234

soldier.''

Two Feathers stepped to No Moon's side. "He is right. There was a time when no Comanche had a horse. The Great Spirit smiled on us and delivered to us our brother, the horse, and we have conquered all the lands where we ride. The time has come to change. We will do as No Moon says.''

"Now, I will explain it once again." He raised his left arm and moved it. "This is the left flank." He repeated the action with his right arm. "The right flank." He pointed to his horse's flank. "Think of it as the flank of your horse. Each of you know if you kick your horse in the flank, he will jump. He will jump because it is a tender place. The same is true when you approach an enemy. His flanks are tender places. If we can hit him in those tender places when he does not expect it, we can crush him like the fox crushes a turkey egg. We can get to the inside and kill our enemy.''

Like the sun comes up, suddenly the braves understood what No Moon had been trying to tell them. His problem was that he had not been talking in terms they could relate to. Now, he was. He started working with smaller groups. He worked every day. The same basic movements over and over again. For over two months, the training went on day after day. He told Gray Dove as they lay wrapped in a buffalo robe, "Tomorrow I will once again put all the braves together and see what they have learned. I have given my word. If this does not work, I will have to leave and go far away.''

She put her finger over his lips. "It will work. You are a leader. It will work.''

When morning came No Moon met Two Feathers and they spoke of small things for several minutes. "It is time to show show the Comanche how he can fight together as one.''

"When?" Two Feathers questioned.

"Today. We will let the sun rise half way, then we will meet in the valley of the red cliffs.''

235

At mid-day, all of the braves were assembled. No Moon and Two Feathers, along with Soaring Eagle, sat on a hilltop overlooking the valley.

"Lord, help this old boy," No Moon said under his breath. He blew on his bugle and the braves rode to their assigned positions. He blew for the attack, then switched the flanks. He blew retreat and then a charge.

He could not believe his eyes. His new troops, the Indian braves who had never fought like this before, functioned like seasoned soldiers. Assembly was called and No Moon and Two Feathers rode down into the flat and met the men. His joy showed on his face.

Two Feathers sat very straight and spread his arms out as he began to speak. "We will ride when the moon has turned full. We will have a feast and prepare ourselves for the greatest battle the Comanche has ever waged on the white man. We will drive him back to where he came from and once again the Comanche will control all these lands that were given to us by the Great Spirit." As Two Feathers finished, No Moon gave a shout and held his bugle over his head.

As Two Feathers said, they had a feast and went through the religious rites of dance and the mixing of paint.

At last the day approached when they would leave on the warpath. No Moon held Gray Dove close as the fire flickered in the tepee.

"Tomorrow I will fulfill my destiny," he said. "Tomorrow we will drive from this land many white men. There will be some of my black brothers there and I will do battle against them also. For this I grieve, but the Comanche must be victorious. All others must die." They sat in silence, then he said, "Should I once again see the cave, the cave where my mother waits, I know I will not return. If this happens, you must promise me not to harm yourself. You must remember the Great Spirit sent me back twice. I can ask no more nor can you. If I do not return, it is because it is the way it must be. If this happens, then you are not to gash your arms or cut your hair." He looked into her eyes and asked, "Do you understand?"

She looked up, tears filling her large brown eyes, "I am Comanche," she said.

No Moon knew no matter what he said Gray Dove would do whatever she had to do for she was Comanche.

Chapter 26

The war party rode out of camp. Many of the warriors had an extra pony as was the custom with some tribes. Two Feathers himself always took an extra mount. The first to ride to battle, the second to ride home.

No Moon rode his big spotted stallion. His chest was bare and the white stripe he had grown accustomed to having on his chest was now twice as wide as it usually was. He had decided this could well be his last battle. He knew the soldiers would keep coming. They would be reinforced with more and more troops. It was only a matter of time before the canyon of arrow wood would be found. Unless they could win a decisive battle, that discovery would probably not be too far in the future. Even with the feeling of ultimate defeat, he had to try to save the Comanche nation.

No Moon had seen part of the great Civil War fought. He had seen soldiers led by great officers, men who would die following orders once committed to a battle plan. He knew all of that yet he had to try to help the Comanche hold on to what was theirs at any cost. Not to try meant no chance at all. This way they at least had some hope of success. There was no one to help the Comanche hold on to what was theirs and as easily as one plucks a flower from a bush, they would be removed from the plains forever.

"This will be a hard battle," he said to Two Feathers.

"It will be, but we will win," Two Feathers answered.

They rode southeast which was where they had seen the fort being built the year before. No Moon felt it would be manned by green, perhaps inexperienced, troops. If it were, they would have better than a fifty-fifty chance of taking the fort. The braves he had trained were seasoned warriors and besides that, they had a reason to win. If they lost, and each understood they might, all would be lost. The very existence of the Comanche, all Indian people for that matter, was at stake on this raid.

Their plan was that after the success of this raid and the collapse of the fort, they would swing westward and sweep the plains clean, voiding it of the white man and the blue coats once and for all.

Word came in from a scout that soldiers had been spotted several miles to the south. It was a party of perhaps twenty troopers and one wagon.

No Moon talked it over with Two Feathers. "If we are lucky that wagon could be carrying supplies needed at the post. If we are very lucky, it could be rifles and ammunition, maybe even some blasting powder."

"We will see," Two Feathers replied.

Scouts were sent out to watch the small detail and they reported back the direction the detail was traveling. The main body of Indians then rode in a circle that would bring the two forces together in a rocky area with low, sharp hills.

The braves reached their position and waited. They spotted the two advance scouts first.

"We have to get those two. If we get them, we'll use their uniforms to decoy the rest into our trap," No Moon remarked. "But we can't use a gun. The shots would just alert the soldiers with the wagon."

Two Feathers signaled for two of his best bow shots. He motioned for them to shoot the advance scouts. The braves disappeared between the large boulders. From their vantage point, No Moon and Two Feathers watched the braves and spotted them from time to time as they worked their way toward the trail.

The Army scouts obviously were seasoned soldiers and with their experience were using extreme caution and taking no chance of being caught off guard. They could feel the danger they were approaching, but did not know from where or when it was coming.

From nowhere it seemed two arrows sang through the air. The two scouts fell from their horses. The horses were caught. No Moon slipped into the uniform of one and another brave put on the other uniform. They then rode back toward the column and waited just far enough away not to be recognized.

When the detail came into sight, they motioned for the column to follow at a quick pace. They turned and both rode out of sight around a bend. No Moon heard the lieutenant in charge call the command, "At a trot! Ho!"

No Moon and his friend stayed just far enough ahead for the lieutenant to get a glimpse of them from time to time, but not close enough to suspect anything. The trick worked just as he had hoped. The column moved between the war party. Before they could retreat, the trap was closed.

When the last shot was fired, three Indians lay dead and two wounded. All of the troopers had been killed. The young braves went about disfiguring the corpses. No Moon had grown used to this now and had convinced himself it was the way things were; maybe not as he would have wanted it to be, but each side tried to outdo the other with the things they did to the dead. "The dead are dead," he told himself. "What is done to a body is only hard on the living. The dead could care less."

He went to the wagon. To his delight there were rifles and ammunition. He looked up and said, "Great Spirit, you smile on us."

One of the troopers who had been wounded managed to see an opening and grabbed a horse. He jumped into the saddle and slammed his spurs into the horse's side. He raced back in the direction from which they had come.

Seven Indians started to follow, but the loose cavalry horses began to follow the trooper. By instinct, the braves tried to catch the horses.

"One bluecoat. What can he do?"

"He is getting away!" No Moon shouted, but his voice went unheard. "He'll get word to the fort. No wonder the Indian is getting the land taken away. He can't change from the old ways. You can't win using the old ways!" he shouted. If anyone heard, they paid no attention.

No Moon then noticed Horse with Short Tail as he made his way clear of the loose horses and followed the escaping trooper. "Sorry as he is, he'll probably catch him." He turned his attention back to the business at hand.

The guns were passed out and bullets were given to all. No Moon found himself with a new rifle. They then rode back toward the east. No Moon hoped the trooper who escaped had headed for another post and not the one they planned to attack. Maybe then they could pull off this attack. If he went to the new fort, the odds just went down. The Army would be ready for them.

When they reached the post, it was almost dark. No Moon had taken a pair of field glasses from the officer in charge of the detail they had ambushed the day before. He wondered again about the trooper who had escaped. Had he reached this fort? Are they on the alert and ready for us? What happened to Horse With Short Tail? These questions crossed his mind as he studied the movement below.

"We've come this far," he said to Two Feathers. "No need to turn back now." He adjusted the uniform and moved down next to the outer wall. From the movement inside the walls, he felt certain the trooper had not reached this post. Otherwise, they would have been preparing for an attack. There would be more sentries on duty. He moved back to where Two Feathers waited.

"We will wait until dawn," he said. He studied the compound using the field glasses. The outer wall was now finished and several buildings were under construction. No Moon spotted something behind one of the buildings. He studied it then realized what it was. It was the rump of a paint horse. The Army only used solid, dark horses, never a paint horse. Horse With Short Tail had been riding a paint.

"That traitor," No Moon said. He handed the glasses to Two Feathers. "Look there," he said and pointed toward the horse.

"Horse With Short Tail," Two Feathers said. "He has been captured."

"Or turned on us," No Moon added.

Two Feathers put the glasses down. "If he did," he said, "I will kill him so slowly your children will grow old before he dies."

"Well, we have to take a chance. The braves are in position and ready." As he spoke, he raised his bugle and sounded the start of the attack.

The right flank rode in and was met with heavy gunfire.

243

He blew the retreat, then ordered a frontal attack, followed by the left flank, then reordered the right flank. It was obvious to No Moon that the post had been warned and was ready. He just had not seen the troops in their concealed positions. Several Indians had been killed, but they held to the attack plan. They had committed themselves and it was too late for a change of plan. They would have to give it all they had and hope the Great Spirit would guide them to victory.

No Moon heard the bugle before they saw the troops. The bugler called for a charge. No Moon saw them as they emerged from the woods about a quarter of a mile away like a blue line. A line of death was closing in on the half-trained Comanche and he knew all was lost. His men were no match for the oncoming cavalry. He blew retreat. He repeated it twice before the Indians caught in the frenzy of war responded. The cavalry had closed the gap and hand-to-hand fighting started.

Two Feathers rode to No Moon's side. "We must go, my brother, or all will be lost." As he shouted, he threw one of the two lances he had carried toward the fort. It was a futile effort but in his mind, he had shown his contempt for the fort and its inhabitants. The braves were now racing for safety. They had scattered like leaves in a windstorm.

No Moon raised his rifle and fired. The bugler fell from his horse. "Maybe that'll slow 'em down some," he said as he kicked his horse into a gallop. The race was on across the flat, barren prairie.

"We must make those hills," Two Feathers called over his shoulder. "It is our only chance."

The braves had fanned out on the prairie, each trying to reach the foothills. They had almost reached the first large boulder that guarded the foothills when Two Feathers' horse fell. A cloud of dust engulfed man and beast. No Moon saw

Two Feathers as he rolled and came up running. He reached down and grabbed him. Two Feathers swung up behind him and the two of them rode into the boulders. The big, spotted horse was winded and started to fall. The added weight was too much for his fighting heart. He stumbled, then fell. Somehow No Moon managed to hang on to his rifle, and by some unknown power, Two Feathers still clung to his second spear. The two men ran into the rocks and concealed themselves. Right behind them ten or twelve troopers dismounted and fired a volley of shots. The two men ducked as the bullets ricocheted off the rocks. No Moon peeked around the boulder behind which he had taken cover. He saw an officer. He took aim and fired. The officer fell backward mortally wounded.

"They got the lieutenant!" someone shouted.

There was silence for ten minutes. No Moon wondered what they were up to. His wait was not long.

"You in there! Black boy. We know you are there and I figure you understand English. Why don't you give it up? You ain't got a chance. Come on out. We promise you a fair trial, just before we hang you."

No Moon looked at Two Feathers. For a moment, the two men felt a message pass between them, yet not a word was spoken.

"You coming out or do we have to come in and get you?" came a shout from the rocks about twenty-five or thirty yards away.

"That's white troops," No Moon said. "That lying Apache may have been telling the truth. Maybe Mackenzie is out here on the plains. If he is, we don't have a chance. I've heard it said he doesn't quit until it's done, no matter what he starts." He took aim and fired. He fired again, then started to reload. He was out of bullets. He threw his rifle down and drew his knife.

"When they come, we'll take as many as we can before they get us," he said. "I'm not going to be taken alive and put in a cage. I'm never going to be put in a cage again. I'll go down fighting and take some of them with me first." Two Feathers knew what the soldiers would do to No Moon if they took him alive. There would be no cage. He would be hung. Two Feathers leaned over toward No Moon and grabbed him around the neck. He shoved his knife deep into his chest. No Moon's face showed surprise and then he relaxed. He smiled and died in Two Feathers' arms. Tears ran down Two Feathers' cheeks. He could not remember when he last wept or if he ever had before.

"My blood brother, you are dead and your spirit is free. It will not be trapped in your body." He knew his cause was dead also. Soon all of his kind would be dead. Two Feathers laid No Moon down. "Now, No Moon, wait for me for soon I will join you at your cave." He leaped to his feet and raced forward, knife in one hand, spear in the other.

A sergeant stood up and leveled his pistol. Two Feathers threw his spear. As it flew through the air, the handgun spoke. The bullet hit Two Feathers in the forehead. His spear was true to its mark also. The sergeant stood for but a moment, his upper body pierced by the second spear of a Comanche warrior.

DOPEFIEND
THE STORY OF A BLACK JUNKIE

BY DONALD GOINES

Donald Goines is a talented writer who learned his craft and sharpened his skills in the ghetto slums and federal penitentiaries of America. **DOPEFIEND** is the shocking first novel by the young man who would go on to write sixteen books; books that made him a household name among readers of black literature.

DOPEFIEND exposes the dark, despair-ridden, secret world few outsiders know about—the private hell of the black heroin addict. Trapped in the festering sore of a major American ghetto, a young man and a girl—both handsome, talented, full of promise—are inexorably pulled into the living death of the hardcore junkie.

DOPEFIEND is an appalling story because it rings so true. It is also a work of rare power and great compassion. **DOPEFIEND** will draw you into a nightmare world you will not soon forget.

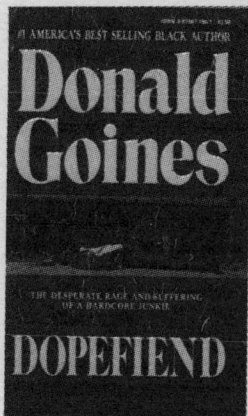

#1 AMERICA'S BEST SELLING BLACK AUTHOR

Donald Goines

THE DESPERATE RAGE AND SUFFERING OF A HARDCORE JUNKIE

DOPEFIEND

KENYATTA'S LAST HIT

BY DONALD GOINES

Ghetto chieftain Kenyatta, the living black legend, concentrates his army's ruthless forces to rid the black community of rampant drug traffic. With the help of Elliot Stone, a black football star and latest recruit to the army, Kenyatta discovers the identity of the number one man...the fat cat king of the drug pushers!

The crack black and white detective team, Benson and Ryan, follow Kenyatta's trail of blood across the country. They're not sure now whether their target is the hated butcher they've believed him to be, or the savior of the black community.

But Kenyatta doesn't give a damn. He has only one goal; the fight to the death with the smack king.

This book is the last in the great Kenyatta adventure series written by the late Donald Goines under the Al C. Clark pseudonym.

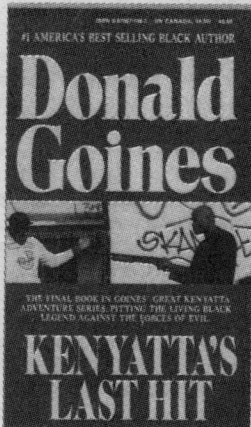

STREET PLAYERS

BY DONALD GOINES

This is Donald Goines' fourth novel, a gutsy account of an Inner City gold-hatted, high-bounding lover. And herein, Goines tests the tensile strength of a ghetto spawn who clawed his way to the top and fights like hell to stay there. He's known as Earl the Black Pearl, and he's up from the ghetto—way up. He views the streets from his fashionable penthouse with its wall-to-wall silk suits and women. He's everybody's mellow fellow, a big spender, the toast of the Inner City. He's as cool and sharp as an ice crystal. Even Joe Chink can't touch him. Then somebody put the heat on. Butcher knives flash and pistols bark, and Earl's friends begin dropping like flies, dragging Earl with them. But he's resilient and he bounces back—for a while...

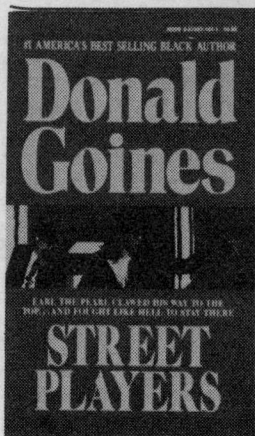

BLACK GIRL LOST

BY DONALD GOINES

Donald Goines has an established reputation as one of the foremost writers in the Black Experience genre. His previous novels have cast a glaring spotlight on the brutally harsh, sometimes nightmarish reality of the ghetto— the cool, clawing world of the pimp in **Street Players**, the cruel, violent conning of ghetto prostitution in **Whoreson**, the treacherous and sordid world of the man behind bars in **White Man's Justice:** **Black Man's Grief**, and the raw, secret world of the black junkie in **Dopefiend**. Now, in **Black Girl Lost**, Goines delves deep into yet another facet of the ghetto existence—the dark, despairing world of a black girl's soul! Sandra took to the streets when she was eight years old, and tried to fight off the hunger pangs by shoplifting. From shoplifting she moved into the profits of pushing drugs as she struggled to overcome her deprivation with quick money. And then she met Chink, and she discovered love and affection...and rape and murder!

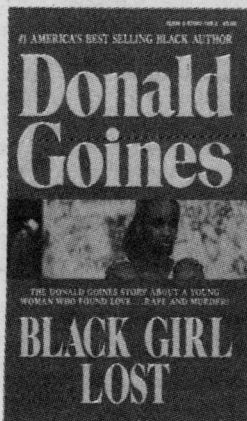

MAMA BLACK WIDOW

BY ICEBERG SLIM

Author Robert Beck, better known by his ghetto pseudonym, "Iceberg Slim," tells the story of Otis Tilson, an incredibly comely and tragic homosexual queen. The dialogue is in the gut idiom of the queer—the black ghetto—the deep South—the underworld—the world of Iceberg Slim, Otis Tilson and his family. It is the story of the black men living in ghetto torture chambers. Men who have been and continue to be niggerized and deballed by the poisonous pus of double standard justice, racial bigotry and criminal economic freeze-out. And of the price paid by their children. In this case, Otis Tilson, his older brother and two beautiful sisters adrift in the dark world of pimpdom and crime and violence. This is Robert Beck's most vivid portrait of ghetto life. A masterpiece!

Iceberg Slim

MAMA BLACK WIDOW

A STORY OF THE SOUTH'S BLACK UNDERWORLD

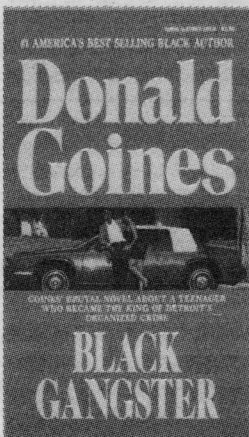

INNER CITY HOODLUM

BY DONALD GOINES

Smack, numbers, money and murder trap a struggling youngblood! Johnny Washington, a teenage Black in Los Angeles, knows the freight yards like the back of his hand. He and his pals Josh and Buddy hit them often, ripping off the boxed up treasures for a fence. They have to. They're the sole support of their families. But when Josh is killed by a trigger-happy security guard and Buddy scatters his brains with nunchaku sticks, they leave the yards for others to try to etch a place in the jungle. Elliot Davis, better known as the Duke, comes to their aid, offering them a place in his ghetto numbers kingdom. But when the Duke recruits Johnny's sister for his stable and later OD's her, Johnny and Buddy come on with a vengeance!

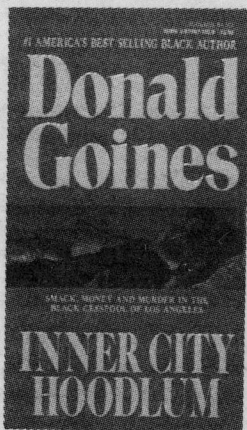